Rane's Giants

Tremble Island Book 1

By Lynn Ray Lewis

ISBN-10# 1-945012-29-3
ISBN-13# 978-1-945012-29-7

Published by Vinvatar Publishing
Website: Vinvatar.com

Table of Contents

Prologue

The crash of the large, silver spaceship went unremarked by the planet's native inhabitants. They were too busy trying to live and provide for their own species to worry about the humans that had survived the crash of the alien aircraft.

The humans had been sent on a mission to establish a colony of humankind on a faraway planet. After three Earth years of exploration, testing soil samples, and looking for vegetation on several planets, the ship had developed several mechanical issues that could not be repaired. All one hundred people on the spacecraft were prepared to die as the ship dropped from space. However, fifty were lucky enough to have survived.

After the initial shock that they had been fortunate enough to land on a planet that was comparable to the one they had left behind, the humans began to establish a small, but growing community for themselves. The longer they lived on this new planet, the more they were able to explore. It appeared to be a doppelganger for Earth. An Earth that no one could imagine. It was a clean environment. There were no factories or large cities. This planet was as virgin as a newborn baby. The humans called the planet Echo.

It wasn't long before the former Earthlings became aware of an amazingly terrifying species that were native to the planet. They were men and women who could shift from a human-like form to an animal. Some were even able to shift into multiple different types of creatures. The humans, in their vast ignorance, shunned these spectacular creatures, calling them monsters, demons, cursed. They weren't willing to accept something, or someone, so completely different from themselves.

The humans began exploring and looking for more space to set up their colonies. Ships were built for the purpose of finding new lands to settle and populate. Hundreds of these expeditions became necessary as the population exploded.

One such expedition brought the settlers to an ideal location. It was an island that seemed to be perfect for their needs. Lush vegetation and beautiful white sand beaches surrounded the bay that they had originally sailed into, and upon further exploration they found mountains, rivers, and several hot mineral springs. Delicious fruits and vegetables were found, as well as, fish and small game.

The explorers began building a village between the lush forest and the mountain range. Everything they could possibly wish for was provided on the island. Plans were made for a return trip to gather families and friends to inhabit the new land. The ship was refitted and would be ready to sail within days.

The farewell celebration was underway when the people felt the earth begin to tremble. Ear-splitting whistles and throaty screams could be heard in the forest surrounding the small encampment. The trembling of the earth and pounding noises continued throughout the night as the animalistic screams and bellows seemed to be coming closer.

Everyone breathed a sigh of relief as a brief silence blanketed them, but that hope was soon shattered as the deafening roar of a big cat sounded close by. The thunderous sound of crashing trees and the shrieks of terrified animals accompanied the bone jarring shaking of the earth as something very large crashed toward the settlement.

Huge gray bodies began crashing through the small encampment. The huts were stomped into the dirt, and the settler's few provisions were destroyed in seconds. The men began to scatter and run toward the beach, as the mountainous creatures got closer to them. Their ship sat in the bay, and was ready enough to sail away from the paradise that had quickly become a nightmare.

Two of the men did not show on the beach, and no one was willing to go back and attempt to rescue their companions. The ship pulled anchor and was drifting out of the bay with the current of the ocean within an hour.

Tremble Island became the new home for any non-human species. It was a dumping ground for the odd or gifted humans. When humans became afraid of them, the beings were shipped to the island.

The hybrid shapeshifters varied from having two forms to having eight forms. The shifters with the most animal forms were usually highly intelligent and became the rulers of the island. Over the years, humans began to be sent to the island. Men and women convicted of any crime were sent to feed the beasts of Tremble Island.

There were few of the giant beasts left on the island. As they died off, none replaced the population. This was a fact that no one shared with outsiders. To the rest of the world, Tremble Island was a wild, barbaric place where humans were food for the beasts. This reputation was enjoyed, and nurtured, by the island's populace.

The current Lord of Tremble Island is Lord Lion. At present, he has five beasts to call to form. Lord Lion shares most of his duties with his brother Lord Nord. They were born just days apart. They were the result of a ménage relationship consisting of their father and his female mates. Since Lion was the first born and has the most animal forms to call, he was declared The Lord Tremble. Nord is his second in command and is also referred to as Lord Tremble.

Though Lord Tremble is the ultimate ruler of the island, the governing of the island is divided into twelve Halls of Care. These halls are split evenly between the humans and the shapeshifters, with the shifters governing six halls, and the humans governing the other six. Only occasionally did Lord Tremble have to step in to resolve a skirmish, or small scale battle, between the different territories.

The Lord Tremble's sire was a highly intelligent man that began opening trade with other countries. The treaties he established with those countries still thrived, and would continue to do so as long as the rules were followed. No shapeshifter or human with power energies could leave the island. Humans were the only species allowed to come and go as trade became the norm.

Welcome to Tremble Island. Where shapeshifters of many forms thrive. A place where those with talents of second sight, and energy are welcome. Odd beings are accepted in this society with open arms.

Chapter 1

Rane finally stopped running, taking refuge behind a trunk in the dungeon of Droildorf Hall. She was on the run from Lord Ludwig's evil brother, Simon. Simon was a horrible, violent man, and after what Rane had just witnessed, and the threat that Simon had issued, she couldn't get away fast enough.

It had only been hours ago that Rane had been caught speaking to, and soothing, Simon's current victim, Della. Della was now pregnant with his child, and she was scared to death. Della had told her of some of his abuse. About how when no one else was around, he had forced Della to take his man part into her mouth, while he grabbed her hair and shoved his cock as deeply as it would go down her throat. No matter how she struggled, he had continued to shove into her mouth, until he finally moaned and shot his load down into her throat.

Della had told Rane that she had not dared to spit it out, or he would have beaten her until she passed out. Della also confessed that she knew her soul was going to the demons for praying the babe would not be born alive. That she was willing to burn with the demons because the Gods and

Goddess had ignored her pleas for help to get away from Simon.

It was during this conversation that Simon had happened upon them. He had heard the last part of Della's sentence, and he was furious. He had pushed Rane away from Della, before curling his fingers into a fist and driving it into Della's face with a sickening crunch of bone.

Rane would have tried to help Della, had Simon not had his minions drag her away.

Simon had turned to her and sneered, "Your next, bitch. Now that she's knocked up I'll need a new toy, and I choose you." He had only laughed as Rane crab-walked backward until her back had hit a wall and she was able to pull herself upright. "Feel free to try and hide."

She didn't look back as she ran. Now she was hiding in the dungeon. It wasn't long enough before she heard a commotion outside the doors.

She peeked around the trunk as the guards brought a prisoner into the dungeon and shackled him to the damp stone wall. Rane knew he would be left to die, just as the three prisoners before him had been. This man was a giant compared to the last one, but his size would not save him. His long brown hair was matted with blood, and his left eye was swollen shut with a nasty bruise. His side showed a long, thin sword wound that blood still seeped from. His chest was decorated with numerous cuts and bruises in varying shades of blue, green, and bright red where the cuts were freshest.

"It is too bad that you will not live to see the fruits of your work today. When you killed Lord Franks, you gifted me with all that was his. As his heir, I am bound to avenge his death with yours. From the way you are bleeding, death will come swiftly," Lord Ludwig hissed.

"It really is convenient that I've captured you, you see. Now the murder of Lord Franks will be blamed on you. It's perfect timing, really. I inherit the Lordship, and you get the blame for a murder that I committed. Thank you for that. It's been a dreadful nuisance pretending to look for a murderer that could have gotten the drop on Lord Franks," the Lord laughed. He stepped over to the prisoner and grabbed a handful of the man's hair, before slamming his head into the stone wall behind him.

The lord finally left with his guards, allowing Rane to breathe a sigh of relief. She had always believed that Lord Ludwig, or Simon, had had something to do with Lord Franks death. Now she knew for certain, and it made her sick to her stomach. Lord Franks had been the one to find her a home, a mother when she had had no one.

Lord Franks had placed her in the home of the village's healer, Old Erma, after she had appeared in the hall around the age of two. All she had at the time was a blue shift, but the Lord had fed her and clothed her. Old Erma told Rane that no one knew where she had come from. The older woman was like a mother to her and they developed a loving bond over the years, as Old Erma taught Rane about medicines and herbs.

It was during those years of learning that they discovered Rane's special gift of healing. This gift had served her well over the years, but it was especially helpful these last few months.

Chapter 2

As soon as Lord Ludwig left she crawled from behind the big chest, and slowly approached the prisoner. He had not moved since they had brought him in. She pulled a large crate over to the giant so she would be able to reach his head. Her hands began to warm as she slowly ran them from the top of his head to the tips of his toes so that she could assess the damage done to his body. She visualized the man's internal injuries and the deep bruising that encompassed his entire body, before setting to work mending the extensive damage.

This man had taken a beating like none before him, and he had not gone down easily. His skull was a web of cracked bone, and three of his ribs were shattered, with another one sticking out from his flesh. Fresh rope burns striped his thickly muscled legs, and his entire body was badly bruised. The stab wound in his gut worried her, but not so much as his fractured skull.

Rane placed her hands on his head over the worst of the man's injuries. She began the tedious task of mending the bone back together, making sure to interlock every small shard of bone so none would be left to float around in his skull after she healed him. Any tiny sliver of bone could cause damage and pain later, so it was better to get the pesky things taken care of the first time and be done with it.

She worked on him for hours, concentrating on knitting his skull back together, and relieving the pressure off his brain. Even if she had water to wash away the blood, and there was a lot of blood, she would not have done it yet. It would take another day, at least, to heal the rest of his injuries enough to remove him from this place, and she would need to gather ashes to place in his current spot for when they escaped. Leaving him a bloody mess would, hopefully, distract the guards from noticing that he was mostly healed.

Rane was getting quite a collection of big men hiding in the cave near the river. Normally when she heard that the Lord had a new prisoner, she slipped into the dungeon through the secret rock in the wall and observed the guards and the Lord, or Simon, come into the room to torture the men for information, or sometimes sport.

When they left the men beaten and shackled at death's door, she would slip through the wall and heal them enough to secret them out of the room, and through the small tunnel leading into the forest.

Today's discovery of a new prisoner was merely a coincidence. She had hid in the dungeon because this was the one place Simon rarely ventured. She again thanked the Goddess for the, smaller than normal, size of her body that had allowed her to hide behind the trunk of torture implements without being detected. There had not been time to hide in the tunnel without being seen by the guards.

That she was already here, in this room, when they brought him in was a blessing for the warrior had he but known it. The bleeding in his brain alone would have killed him after days of torturous pain. That is, of course, if he hadn't bled out from the stab wounds, or the rib sticking out of his chest.

Rane took her hands from the warriors head. The rest would have to wait until tomorrow. At least, the huge man was still incapacitated from the severity of his wounds, and the healing. That, along with all the blood, would help convince the guards that he would be dead soon. Hopefully, they wouldn't notice that the blood had stopped seeping from his wounds. They often took bets on how long a prisoner would bleed before they died.

It puzzled her as to why this warrior, and the past three like him, had not been killed outright on the battlefield as so many had been. Nor had they been subjected to the lord's usual depravities. For some reason, he seemed to fear these men, and when a small pile of ashes had been found where the prisoner had been chained, all he did was grunt and nod his head. He ordered his guards to sweep up every ash and scatter the ashes into the wind over the fields.

Lately, when the lord felt particularly like he needed entertainment, and there were no prisoners already in the dungeon, he would have a villager brought into the hall on a trumped up charge. He would then watch as his men tortured the poor soul. The villagers were raped, and beaten. One man had been strung up over the blackened beams overhead and roasted over a vat of bubbling fat. His screams were said to still echo in the hall on cold nights.

Sadly by the time each villager was tossed out of the hall like a pile of garbage, if still alive, their mind was too broken for Rane to heal them. She might heal their bodies, but the mind was in the hands of the Goddess.

The younger villagers had begun fleeing from Droildorf in the middle of the night in pairs and small groups. No one was safe in this place anymore. Parents were helping as best they could to get their progeny out of harm's way, as the refugees were said to have been allowed to build lives and shelters if they found their way to the castle of Lord Tremble.

It was said to be a haunted place with a violent past, but the villagers made good livings by fishing and were encouraged in artisan works.

Some of the younger people that had made it to Tremble Castle found a way to come back and sneak their older relatives away to the new life that they had made. The former occupants of Droildorf Village thrived in their new situation, and Rane was happy for them. Perhaps one day she would leave and beg the Lord Tremble to allow her to ply her trade as a healer in his village.

For now, she needed to leave the dungeon and ground the pain that she had taken from the warrior. She could feel it pushing from the corner in her mind. Until she released the pained energy into the flowing water, or another person, it would hammer at her brain until she was blind with the pain that she took from another.

She briefly thought of gifting Simon with the pain, but that daydream was quickly rejected. To cause him pain, and not kill him, would be a death sentence. Her life was too precious to throw it away on a lowly, evil cretin such as him. If he were to attack her that would be an entirely different circumstance, but she would be forced to leave immediately and find her way to a new life elsewhere.

"Warrior, hear me," she whispered, "I must leave you now, but will return soon. I have healed the direst of your wounds as best I can for now. Use the time for healing sleep. I promise to return."

Rane stifled a groan as she stood. Her muscles burned from holding the position in front of the warrior for so long. She crawled to the opposite wall and climbed on a rock sitting on the floor. Before pushing inward on a hidden stone, she sent out feelers to make certain no one was around to witness her departure from the dungeon.

By the time she made her way to the cave, that was housing the five other men in various states of healing; she was exhausted. She was forced to stop and immerse herself in the river to allow the pain to flow out of her and into the strong current. Then she had to catch enough fish to feed the men since she did not have the time to snare several hares for the men to eat.

Thankfully, the water ritual helped energize her so she could keep going up the rocks, especially now that she was burdened with the large catch of fish for the men.

The man called Nord was sitting behind a rock ready to trounce anyone who may discover the hidden cave. He plucked the sack from her fingers and hauled her up by the arm over the large rocks.

The huge sword at his back was something Rane had found while searching the sites of the battles for men who might still be alive. She had hidden several swords and dirks in the cave over the years. Now she knew that the urge to hide the weapons came to her from the Goddess.

It was on two of her recent forays into the darkness that she had found the other two men. She knew she would need help moving the warrior from the dungeon. One of these men would be enough, she hoped, to help her carry the huge man through the tunnel and woods to the cave.

After seeing to the broken leg of the man the others called Mouse, and tending the other's various injuries, she knew that they were just about ready to make their way back home. She never asked them where they came from, because it didn't matter to her. As long as their enemy was her enemy they were worth using her talents on and risking her life.

Mouse and Nord began cleaning the four large fish that Rane brought to them. There were only potatoes, and four heads of cabbage left on the rocks near the fire, so the fish would be a good change of meal for the men.

She decided to tell the men about the giant warrior in hopes that, at least, one would volunteer for the dangerous rescue mission. She knew that if she asked one to help there was no way he could refuse her request. A volunteer knew the consequences but wanted the job anyway. That was what she needed.

"They brought another of your brethren into the dungeon today. He was, and still is, in dire straits. The man is a giant. He has dark brown hair. I did not see his eyes. He does have a large tattoo on his back, but I did not see the whole thing because he is too big and heavy for me to move on my own. I would guess that Lord Ludwig lost more than a few soldiers when they tangled with the warrior.

"If I had not started to heal him before I left, he would soon die of brain swelling, blood loss, or infection. I did as much for him as I possibly could. I overheard Lord Ludwig tell the man that his death would be the vengeance for Lord Franks' death, but that it was only to appease those who were still looking for Lord Franks' murderer. Lord Ludwig said that he himself had been the one to kill Lord Franks."

As soon as she mentioned the size of the warrior, the men before her began to stand. Even Mouse with his broken thighbone tried to rise. At the mention of the tattoo they began to gather weapons. From the way they were reacting, she could only guess that these men knew, and respected, the wounded warrior. She would not need to ask for volunteers. She would be forced to deny all but one of them direct participation in the rescue of their injured comrade.

Nord was the fittest of the men, and his injuries had been the least dire, when Rane found him in the dungeon. The only problem with taking him was the fact that he was nearly as big as the warrior that needed to be rescued.

She remembered her first sight of Nord. The man had been sitting against the wall of the dungeon, with a cracked skull. She had been forced to straddle his thighs in order to reach her hands to hold his head. Her body seemed to hum, and her belly tightened as the heat radiating from his huge body warmed her, making it very difficult to concentrate on healing his injuries. She blushed as she remembered the way her nipples had hardened just from her nearness to the big man. When his thick prick hardened, and rose between the cradle of her thighs, the feelings became more intense. She had drawn her hands back from his head to find his intense blue eyes staring at her. Surprised, she had scrambled from his lap and landed on her rear end on the floor.

He had taken the knife that she had brought with her and released the shackles from his wrists and ankles. As they made their way through the tunnel, he had been forced to shimmy his huge body to get through the passage. His shoulders had been badly scraped by the time they had reached the outside of the tunnel.

Shaking out of her memories, she addressed the men.

"Nord, I have no doubt of your abilities to help, but I need to take someone smaller into the tunnel with me so there will be room enough for three of us to pass through. The man is not just big; he is a giant. I planned only to take one of you with me to get him out, but, Nord, can help us carry him when we reach the outside of the passage."

Drago, Max, Hawk, and Nord stood in front of her. It was a solid wall of overdeveloped muscular flesh. Mouse was still struggling to rise until Nord said something to him under his breath. His voice was so low that even Rane's sensitive hearing could not catch the command. Mouse immediately stopped his struggles and sank back down with a resigned look on his face.

"I will go into the tunnel with you, Lady Rane," Max offered. "Hawk will guard our path, and Drago will have our backs," he gestured to the men as he spoke to her, "Nord and I will carry our Lord Tremble if need be."

The men started for the entrance of the cave, but Rane had to stop them.

"The path is treacherous in the dark as you all know, and if we go now someone could see us and report to Lord Ludwig. Right now he thinks you have died and turned to ash in his dungeon. If you are seen before we rescue your Lord, then he will be killed without delay. He is a sadistic man, and would make the death a very painful one. We must wait."

The men conceded, yet continued to prowl around the small space. They were flexing their muscles and scowling, the wait obviously wearing on their nerves. Unfortunately, there was nothing Rane could do about it. She found a patch of soft dirt near the back wall and sat to meditate. The name of the giant was familiar.

Wait, Lord Tremble? The Lord Tremble? As in, Lord of Tremble Castle, where most of the fleeing villagers had settled?

Why would they come to Droildorf? From all accounts, Tremble had everything this place did not. There was nothing here to attract anyone, except fighting. Rane did not realize she had spoken the questions out loud until Nord came and sat in front of her while Hawk flanked him.

"Why did we come? Do you have any idea the number of refugees that have come to Tremble by the Sea in the past few months? We are running out of room for them all. Droildorf is not the only sector with a vicious overlord, but your Lord Ludwig stands out from the crowd of tyrants."

Chapter 3

Nord took up the conversation as Hawk got up and stomped to the entrance of the cave.

"Lord Tremble cannot bring himself to turn away the refugees, but it is getting to the point where a man cannot walk five steps in any direction without tripping over another person. No one is allowed to laze around at Tremble Castle. We've had to manufacture positions for all of the new people. We have run out of options to keep the additional people productive.

"We were sent to negotiate with four lords, one of them is now breathing dirt. Lord Ludwig did not give us a chance to negotiate, or even speak before the treacherous bastard attacked. I still have no idea what happened to my men. I suspect that they have all been murdered. If that is what has happened, there will be hell to pay.

"Ludwig's followers will be put to death as surely as he will be. Lord Tremble must have been concerned about the delay in our return, and has come himself to investigate. If I had to guess, I would say that he allowed himself to be taken so he could find us. He is unmatched in battle," Nord said reverently. "No petty little tyrant could have brought him low unless he allowed it to happen.

"Now, Lady Rane, it is time for us to leave. Darkness is falling, and I would like to get my Lord Tremble out of that place without further delay."

It seemed that her small army of patients was taking over, and she was happy to let them. Rane was tired but knew it would be hours before she could allow herself to rest. Goddess knew what would happen once they got back to Lord Tremble. His name certainly fit him as far as she could tell.

The man was a giant in size. She would wager that many people would tremble just from seeing him come their way. His face was square and his nose was straight. While she had not seen the color of his eyes, she could remember that they had not been spaced so close together as to look cross-eyed. His body was magnificent, despite the bruising and other injuries.

The men made their way through the rocks with an ease that Rane envied. Nord insisted on carrying her on his back most of the way to the tunnel. He told her that she was slowing them down and that she needed to conserve her energy to heal Lord Tremble when they got to the dungeon.

Hawk and Drago split off from the group to make certain the path was cleared. The beautiful hawk, sitting high in the pine tree that marked the entry to the tunnel, made Rane stop in her tracks. She knew that the bird must be Hawk. It would be too great a coincidence otherwise.

She stood frozen as she looked at Nord and Max. She wanted to hear it for herself. If Hawk was indeed a shapeshifter, what about the others? Drago? Was he a dragon?

Rane could see that Nord had caught on to her train of thought. It would be hard not to with her eyes darting between all of them. Unfortunately, she also knew that the men were anxious to get to their lord, and would not appreciate another delay. It was also possible that the men would need to shift later. Did shifters need to conserve energy like she did? Did it take a lot for them to shift?

She couldn't stop thinking about her discovery of the men as shape-shifters. Mouse? Goodness, he was the smallest of the men, but not small enough to be a mouse. But then Hawk was a large man, and even though the bird was large, it was not in any way proportionate to his body size. She tried to picture Nord as an animal, but he was almost as big as her warrior. What kind of- Wait. Her warrior?

That thought was too confusing for her to wrap her brain around right now. She already had enough to worry about attempting to keep them all alive.

Before she slipped under the round rock near the thick trees, Nord took her aside.

"Lady Rane, we need to talk about something that I have hesitated to bring up because I have not wanted to offend, or scare, you. I can't go into detail at present, but please, do as I say. When you go to Lord Tremble, you will need to give him the gift of a few sips of your blood. It is the one sure way to arouse him from any injury, and it will help him heal very quickly."

Rane was astonished to learn that something as easy as giving a man her blood would result in a quicker recovery for the warrior. It even made sense in a strange way. Animals needed bloody meat, right? Was this man asking her to sacrifice her life for Lord Tremble's?

"I can see that you have drawn the wrong conclusion. I would never do you harm, nor would I ask you to sacrifice your life for that of my brother's, Lord Tremble. I am not asking for your life small one," his voice was soothing, and his eyes were sincere. "Here, give me your hand for a moment, please."

When she complied, his large hand cradled her small one as his thumb slowly rubbed over her pulse. He brought her wrist to his lips leaving a kiss on the fine blue veins showing through her skin.

"Say the words as I tell you to say them. My life. Take my gift. Know that I am with you. Take my life, my gift. Know my heart is true."

Rane stumbled over the words the first time she spoke them. Nord had her say them again, and yet another time, before he brought her wrist back to his mouth. She watched as, needle thin, spikes descended from his gums and penetrated her skin.

She could feel the blood being pulled from her vein. At first, she felt fear, but that didn't last but a fleeting second before she wanted to toss her head back in pleasure. She hoped the feeling never stopped. She felt a strange sense of abandonment when Nord's fangs withdrew from her. His tongue licked the skin where his fangs had penetrated. The small sizzle sealing her skin barely registered. She wanted him to take more, but he let her arm go and took a step back from her.

She couldn't contain her whimper at the loss of contact.

The call from the hawk high above brought them all to attention. Nord urged her to get in the tunnel and Max quickly followed before the rock was pushed back into position.

The journey through the tunnel was slow going. There were twists and turns before another sliding rock blocked the tunnel so if someone inside the compound ever discovered it, it would appear to be one of three dead ends. It was also the narrowest section of the tunnel. When they entered the larger area where the three offshoots split, they had to be very quiet.

Max crawled next to her, and they could hear yelling, and cursing, on the other side of the rock.

"Damn you, you will not die as the others have. You will heal enough to tell me the secrets of your master, Lord Tremble. How does he stay young and hearty? What causes his loyal men to turn to ash upon death? Already you have begun to shrink just like the others before you. I demand to know the secret before I allow you to die. I have sent for the healer and will have her revive you long enough to tell your secrets to me. Only then will I grant you a less painful death. If you refuse, you will be burned alive."

Rane recognized Simon's voice. She wondered why his brother, Lord Ludwig, was not there with him harassing the unconscious prisoner.

The next conversation that they overheard was between Simon and his minion, Melvin. It made her blood run cold.

"Well, where is she? Do not tell me that you have not found her yet," Simon let out a string of curses. "She is small but she cannot hide from our finest soldiers."

Of course, they were looking for her. She was the only healer left in the village since Old Erma had passed.

"I personally searched the hall, and village for her, Simon. She is nowhere to be found. Also, something strange is happening. It looks, to me, as if half the villagers have vanished. I torched the hovel that she stays in, so she will have no choice but to come to the hall for a safe place to sleep tonight. I have sent out two patrols to search the forest, and the outbuildings, for her and the missing villagers. They cannot have gone far, especially with the night being as dark as pitch.

"Oh, and your brother is now missing an additional old woman from the village," his tone suggests he couldn't care less. "She swore that she had no knowledge of Rane's whereabouts. She also claimed to know nothing about the missing villagers. She died while I was questioning her," Melvin chuckled softly. "Yeah, the old bitch fell and hit her head on the stone hearth in her hut. It was the strangest thing."

The woman had not fallen. His filthy hands had probably knocked the woman's head into the hearthstones.

Melvin was known for molesting things smaller than him. He had raped one of the village women last year, right in the middle of town. He didn't discriminate in his vile endeavors. The general consensus was that Melvin liked women best, but if one was not handy, a man would serve his purpose just as easily.

"Then, I guess, I need to go to the village and make certain that they know that we will not tolerate sneaking around. When the patrols find the missing villagers, bring them before me, or Lord Ludwig. We will set an example of them tomorrow after the evening meal. It's obvious that we need to teach these churls their place.

"I will join the search for Rane. First, she will heal this sorry excuse for a human being. Then, I will claim her for all to see. The secrets of Tremble shall be mine as surely as the witch will be."

Rane grew even more concerned for her own safety. Simon had always left her alone, like every other man in the area had. Despite the care that she had taken, she was still considered a witch, therefore untouchable. She would rather die than become Simon's toy. The man was as depraved as any vicious animal. He must have decided to take his chances with her reputation.

A vow to stop him from harming her, or anyone else, settled over her shoulders. She would kill him if he attacked her. Her new resolve made her swallow her fear. The goddess could not help her once she took his life, she would be executed for her actions.

The thick door was slammed shut, and the iron bolt shot across to keep the room secure. Max started for the rock blocking the entrance into the dungeon, but Rane put her hand on his arm stopping him. When he went to speak she put a finger to her lips and shushed him. Seconds later they heard the bolt being drawn back and the door opening. Leather boots scraped softly across the stone floor of the dungeon, before Lord Ludwig's voice boomed through both spaces, demanding the secrets of Tremble Castle.

"My brother thinks to make a fool of me by extracting the knowledge of Tremble's strength and youth from you before I can. He will pay for that indiscretion with his life, but not before I allow him to abuse and torment you as he wishes.

"I find myself admiring you which disturbs me. Not that that will save you, of course. You will die, whether by our hands, or the way of your people, by fire."

After the door was closed and the bolt shot to lock the door, Rane removed her hand from Max's arm indicating that it was safe to go through the portal.

Rane bit her lips to keep from crying out at the condition of the warrior's face. Long, thin ribbons of blood scored his cheeks, and the former straight bridge of his nose was now sitting off center.

She forced herself to breathe evenly as her hands ran over his body searching out any new injuries. The damage to his face was the only recent abuse that she could find. Rane promptly laid one hand delicately over his broken nose, as her other hand went to the sliced flesh of his cheeks. His rib still needed to be set. He needed to be prone so she could wrap it into place while the bone knitted back together.

There were just too many injuries for her to heal at once, each as necessary as the next to aid his recovery. Rane felt a tinge of defeat before she remembered what Nord had instructed her to do. She pulled a small dirk from her belt, sliced a shallow cut in her wrist, and held it to his lips. When his fangs did not drop, and his mouth did not clamp on her skin, she pried his lips apart. Her blood was barely showing along the thin line of the cut, so she let him go and gouged deeper into her flesh with the dirk before quickly holding it to his, still open, lips. She watched closely as the blood dripped into his mouth, holding her breath for any change.

She didn't have to wait long. Almost immediately, the needles dropped and sank into the cut. Rane was thankful for the dim lighting, as her nipples hardened and her belly tightened. She had felt this earlier with Nord, but the feelings were still a shock. The liquid that started leaking out of her, from between her thighs, was still a shock. Her confusion helped to snap her out of the sensual fog that she had fallen into.

She pulled herself together and spoke the words that Nord had forced her to memorize.

For several, long minutes Lord Tremble pulled at her vein. Rane could feel his body coming alive under her hands. She sat back on her calves and bowed her head, attempting to make the dizziness go away. They were not safe and, although he was rousing, the warrior still had a ways to go to heal completely. There was nothing more that she could do for the giant warrior right now.

Ignoring her exhaustion, Rane signaled for Max to help her with the shackles. Max used his knife and bare hands to snap the cuffs from Lord Tremble's limbs. They worked together to get the giant on his feet, but Rane was no match for the strength that Max displayed. Her head barely met the lord's armpit, so using her shoulders to help prop him up was a waste of time and energy.

Max stood the man's body on his knees and then crawled into the mouth of the tunnel. Then he reached out and pulled the Lord's arms up and into the tunnel with him. Rane stood behind the wounded man and kept him as upright as possible to help Max pull the giant to safety.

She looked around the dungeon, making sure that they left nothing behind, before remembering that she needed to pile ashes where the warrior had been shackled. Reaching into the tunnel she snagged a small cloth sack. She poured the ashes onto the ground and spread them over a small space. She arranged the shackles just so before slipping back into the tunnel, and sliding the stone back into position.

Chapter 4

Drago huffed a sigh of satisfaction, as he watched the broken body of the last of the four guards bounce off the roof of Droildorf Hall, and land at the front entrance doors. It would be a nice surprise for the inhabitants come morning.

The small group had been attacked while making their way back to the cave by the river, but the four soldiers hadn't been a problem. They were dead within minutes, and Drago happily volunteered to dispose of the bodies, while the others got Lord Tremble to safety.

For curiosity's sake, and to ease Lady Rane's concerns, he flew over the village. He watched as six soldiers roused each hovel and came out of each with either nothing or one or two occupants. The people were being thrown into a small animal pen.

On silent wings, he glided closer to the group of soldiers. Upon further investigation, he noticed that one of the men was no soldier, he was a nobleman. A pitiful specimen of manhood in the dragon's estimation. The little, pretentious prick would burn as bright as the others.

When the last hovel had been searched, the older woman that had been dragged out was tossed into the dirt at the nobleman's feet only to be repeatedly kicked as he yelled abusive words at her. Drago finally allowed his dragon free reign.

At first, no one knew what was happening. It wasn't until two men began to run and scream, after becoming human torches, that the others looked around. Nobody even thought to look to the skies for the danger.

The dragon swooped in, letting his fire incinerate two more soldiers. As he set fire to a couple more, he snatched up the nobleman, as well as, the man standing at his side. He flew them around enjoying the screams and cries of the men for a short time. Deciding to drop the soldier with his fallen comrades, he rose high above the hall dropping the screaming man on top of the hall, and watching as the body crashed through the roof into the second floor, where the sleeping chambers were situated.

The nobleman was pleading to be spared, but when Drago felt the pinprick of a knife blade try to penetrate the thick scales covering his leg, he looked for a spot to land. He decided on the middle of a small vegetable patch, and set them down, folding his wings behind him.

The nobleman was under the talons of the dragon, as the dragon proceeded to tear off limbs beginning with the arms. The man screamed in excruciating pain until he began to choke on his own blood. He laid there missing both arms as the dragon began tearing at his leg to remove it. The man finally stopped screaming, passing out from the pain. The lack of noise calmed the dragon before he began to hear cries coming from the direction of the hall. He decided to take what was left of the evil man back to his protectors.

The occupants of the hall swarmed from the building. Lord Ludwig was one of the first to leave the great entrance. He stood in a patch of dirt, gazing at the sky, as if, waiting for more bodies to fall, or something worse. The sight of several dead bodies lying broken over the slate rooflines of the hall was a gruesome sight that Drago was quite proud of.

Hardened soldiers were panicking, looking to Lord Ludwig for guidance. However, his attention was on the flaming ball of flesh falling rapidly toward them. When the body landed not twenty feet away from the lord, he advanced. He fell to his knees at the sight of his younger brother's melting face, frozen in terror for all time.

Drago watched as Lord Ludwig hurried back inside the hall followed by the last of his soldiers. They didn't surface for the remainder of the night in the great hall.

When the darkness of the night was chased away by the bright light of morning, Lord Ludwig ordered all ten of his remaining men to come outdoors with him before breaking their fast. No one seemed inclined to argue, or hide, from the gruesome tasks that awaited them.

The soldiers removed the bodies from the rooftop, and Simon's body was rolled onto a length of sheeting. A lone soldier carried the body of Melvin from inside the hall, and laid it beside Simon. The villagers brought the charred bodies of the other four soldiers from the night before. Ten shrouds lay in a row. Ten men that would only be missed by ten men just like them, and a lord that knew his days were numbered.

Lord Ludwig stood over the bodies and questioned the ragged few that had witnessed the tragedies. No one actually saw anything, although one old man from the village claimed to have seen a river of fire from the sky hit the soldiers. Then darkness had pulled Simon, and Melvin, into the black void of the sky, screaming as they disappeared.

Drago watched the proceedings and chuckled to himself, before taking off to join the others at the cave and check on Lord Tremble.

****

Max offered to carry Rane back to the cave, but she resisted.

"You cannot touch me, nor I you, until I get out of the water of the river. To have my touch after I use my gifts of healing, is to share the pain of the person I have given aid to."

She didn't want the men to fear her touch, but they needed to understand the gravity of the situation.

Nord passed Lion to Hawk and Max when they reached the river. He sent them ahead, waiting while Rane cleansed Lion's pain from her system. A small argument began when Rane insisted that Nord leave her alone for the time it took to deal with her ritual. Eventually they came to a truce that stated that Nord could stay as long as his back was turned while she was naked in the water.

"Lady Rane, perhaps I was not clear when I told you about the sharing of your life's blood with Lion and myself. Did you not understand the meaning of the words you spoke?" His tone was more self-deprecating, than accusing, and it helped to ease Rane's temper.

When Rane came out of the water, she quickly donned her clothing and came around the rock he sat on. She looked up at him questioningly, patiently waiting for an explanation.

"The words, Lady. Remember the words. You spoke them freely. It is too late to change your mind now, especially since you have said them not only to me, but to my brother Lord Lion, also known as Lord Tremble of Tremble Castle by the Sea."

Rane thought through the words, 'My life, take my...'

Oh, Goddess. She looked at Nord as she comprehended what he was telling her.

"The words mean that I have given myself to you and Lord Lion?" He nodded and gave her a small smile. "I have bound my life with the two of you?"

****

She looked so lost that Nord pulled her to him, settling her on his lap. His thick arms came around her and urged her head back onto his shoulder. She was so small that he wondered what the Gods were thinking to pair her with him and his brother. There was no question that she belonged to them. From the moment she first touched him he knew she was destined to be theirs.

The family curse, or gift, depending on how you wished to look at it, said that the brothers would share a love. They would have children with that love, and be healed of pain by that love. If the brother's allowed jealousy to come between them, the love would wither and die. Should that happen, the brothers would know untold pain and sorrow.

Nord had suspected she was the one when he first saw her. Then the gentle caress of her delicate fingers confirmed it. The gift of her blood sealed her fate. The fact that he had felt energized with the first sips of her blood, instead of becoming sick to his stomach, coupled with his intuition, was enough proof for him. He could take blood donations from other males, but only a potential mate could share her blood between the brothers without them becoming very ill. She was theirs now. Lion would be especially happy to finally have found their wife. In fact, Nord was looking forward to seeing his brother's expression when he realized that the little one was theirs.

She was such a pretty little thing, with light brown hair, and the most amazing green eyes. Her height was presently a deterrent, but once he and Lion completed the bonding ritual her shape might very well change.

He did not care if she changed size for his comfort, he rather liked her petite form, with her wide hips and full breasts. No, the change that would come was for her comfort. A woman as small as Rane could be crushed between the brothers very easily. Not to mention that their cocks were proportionate to their size.

Right now, she sat on his lap needing reassurance.

"I thought you understood the words when I had you repeat them so many times. You have been destined to be ours since the moment you saved me from the Lord's dungeon. The prophecy that Lion and I were told is complicated, but simply put, we will share a love that will be the mother of our children, and the healer of our bodies and souls. She will meld the three of us together so tightly that there will be no room for jealousy, or hurt feelings, between us.

"Should one begin to feel the claws of jealousy, then all will be lost. Our love will wither and die, and we will be alone, and in excruciating pain, for all time." Nord hugged her tighter, and waited for her response.

41

****

Rane tried to think. There was a lot to think about. It seemed that she had, by her own ignorance, given her life to the Brothers Tremble. The idea was hard to absorb. How was this supposed to work?

"I cannot see how this will work, Nord. The two of you are giants. I am not nearly a large enough woman to deal with your-," she paused, she blushing bright red, as she searched for words, "manly needs. Are you certain that this is our destiny? I had never thought to be wed, let alone to two giants such as yourself and Lord Lion."

Rane startled as Nord bent down and kissed her lips. Her surprised gasp quickly turned to a hum as she began to accept the feeling of his kiss.

His hands ran at will over her squirming body, while his lips kept her mouth occupied in a deep, open mouthed, kiss. His large hands weighed her plump breasts, before his fingers started to lightly pinched at her nipples. He did this over and over, until she broke the kiss and put her arms over his shoulders.

When his hands abandoned her breasts, she whimpered. Then she felt her dress being lifted up past her thighs. He spread his legs, which in turn spread hers. His mouth came down on hers again as she felt a thick finger trail through the curls of her sex. The finger wandered to the small nub at the top of her slit and when it began to rub on the spot, she cried out into his mouth as the kiss continued.

He raised his head, looking into her startled, lust filled eyes.

"You will see that making love is not as bad as you are expecting little one. I am going to give you a taste of what we will do for you to make you happy. Lie back against me, and enjoy the feel of my fingers in your sweet pussy.

"Do you feel my finger on your little clit? That is just one of your pleasure centers. Let me see if I can find more, okay?" His fingers trailed along her lower lips, "How about this one? This is where my cock will join our bodies together." His pleasured groan matched her own.

"Your entrance is so tight that you will squeeze my prick until I beg for mercy. Now, I will push my finger inside of you just like my cock will when the time comes. Your sweet pussy is gushing cream to ease my way."

She was too far gone to be embarrassed over her wetness, but a bright blush still stole over her at his words.

"That is a good thing, little one. When your pussy gives me this much cream, it means that it wants me to slide into this gorgeous, pink flesh."

Rane heard Nord weaving the words of enticement into her ear, and loved the feelings that his voice was creating deep within her. The feeling of wetness coming from her body made her think of what happened while she was healing Lion and giving him her blood. She knew now, that her body was readying itself to take him inside.

The sensations his finger was causing in her were breathtaking.

His finger began to slide in and out of her delicate flesh, and all she could do was to sit and enjoy the pleasure. He dragged moisture up and over the small knot of nerves that he called her clit, slipped back inside of her opening, then repeated the pattern over and over until she was moving her hips in rhythm with his finger. Rane let out a low moan, as the burning in her body grew to a fever pitch.

When he added a second finger into play, while using his other hand to cup her breast and play with her nipple, she forgot all about being quiet.

The cheeks of her ass were spread, and his cock swelled to unfathomable proportions, as she moved her hips back against him. His words of encouragement added to the foreign pleasure, as his fingers began to glide faster, and the fingers playing with her nipples pinched harder.

"Can you feel how your little pussy clings to my fingers as they slide deep inside of you? Can you feel how my finger loves to kiss your clit? My cock is jealous, as are my lips. You see, my cock wants to be buried inside of you," he whispered into her ear, as he pushed two fingers deep, while his thumb slid over her clit. "And my lips and tongue long to lick and suck on your nipples. The next time we are together like this, my lips will roam freely over your beautiful body. My tongue will lick the cream from your pussy, and then I will fuck you as deep as I can get inside your snug depths. Wouldn't you like that, dear one?"

When his fingers pinched down hard on her nipple, she couldn't stop the scream that came from deep within. Her brain was showing such a burst of colors that she wept from the pleasure. She could not stop her hips from moving as she rode out her pleasure on his fingers, all the while, thrusting back against the hard ridge between the cheeks of her ass. Her body bowed, and she whimpered as the pleasure kept coming in little waves, until all she could do was twitch. His fingers withdrew and she slumped back onto his wide chest.

****

Nord pulled her knees together, and smoothed her skirt down to cover her legs. He held her for long minutes, until finally hearing her deep, steady breathing that indicated she was asleep. He gathered her into his arms and carried her to the cave, where he laid her down on a pallet of soft furs.

He checked on Lion, noticing that much of the bruising on his face was gone. Hawk and Max had set the rib back into place, and wrapped a length of cloth around him to hold the rib where it belonged. Drago finally arrived, and Nord wondered at the grin on the man's face, but said nothing.

He laid his weary body down beside Rane and closed his eyes. Morning light was already breaking, but he needed some rest before taking the day's tasks.

Chapter 5

Lion woke to the taste of blood being siphoned into his system. From the taste, it was Drago that was his donor. He felt a strange tingling in his body, that had nothing to do with the blood Drago was giving him, and he pulled back from the wrist at his mouth. He automatically licked the wound to seal it.

When he opened his eyes, Drago was smiling at him from above his prone position. He tried to sit up, but fell back groaning at the pulling in his ribs.

"My friend, you might want to take it easy for a few minutes. You have a broken rib that Hawk and Max reset last night. They wrapped it to hold it in place. The stab wound has almost healed, as has, your skull, that from what I hear, was crushed in. Rest easy, I will get Nord. He can explain everything to you," Drago grinned widely. "One thing is for sure, this has been an interesting adventure, and it's not over yet."

Whatever Drago was talking about must be amusing him greatly, because Drago rarely smiled like that. He was normally stoic. It was too much to contemplate, at this time, as Lion felt an almost desperate need to get up and relieve himself before he was truly labeled an invalid.

Lion grasped the arm that Drago held before him to pull up into a sitting position. From there, after a few moments of gasping for breath, he allowed Drago to assist him to stand. Drago continued to stand by his side to ensure that Lion could stand and move on his own with no mishaps.

"Why do I feel like I have been buried beneath a pile of heavy stones? My head bangs like some demented gnome is beating a drum inside of it, and my ribs feel bruised. If I do not empty my bladder soon, we will have a flood in this cozy cave. Direct me to the doorway, Drago."

After Lion finished watering the rocks a few feet from the cave, he slowly turned around in a tight circle, getting his bearings, and enjoying the view. The dense forest was beautiful this time of year, showing off the differing greens and reds of the leaves for anyone who appreciated it enough to notice.

He could hear the swift current of water rushing over rocks and downed trees, and knew they must be close to a river. He spied Hawk sailing up over the rocks with a large salmon in his talons, and smiled as the huge bird dropped the fish at his feet, before it turned back for more prey.

The wolf sitting on the rocks above their rustic home was on guard, while basking in the sunlight. He looked as if he didn't have a care in the world, but Lion knew from experience that it would take a great deal of stealth to get past the wolf's ears and eyes. Max was indeed an asset to any group of soldiers.

Mouse was sitting upright when Lion came back into the cave with the large fish.

"I will clean it, Lord Lion, it is not like I have been much help since Lady Rane brought me from the dungeon. My leg is almost healed, but she insists that I sit or lie around all day, not putting any weight on it. Lord Ludwig tried to remove my leg on the rack. He didn't succeed, but the bone broke in a very painful way. While he was distracted, Lady Rane got me out of there, and brought me here, with the help of Lord Nord and Drago."

Drago huffed as he returned without Lord Nord, or Lady Rane.

"Lady Rane insisted on going to the village to help the people that are left in that squalor. Lord Nord is watching over her while she tends to them.

"Lord Ludwig is currently planning the funerals for his dead, one of which is his younger brother, Simon. No one is grieving for the men lying in the hole that Ludwig ordered the villagers to dig. Unfortunately for him, or I should say, his soldiers, there aren't any able bodied villagers left. His own soldiers are finishing the digging, while the villagers gather firewood for a funeral pyre. He plans to incinerate the bodies sundown.

"The dead were killed in three ways. Four were burned to death, two died from undetermined causes, two bled to death, one fell to his death, and Simon was on fire and missing limbs when he fell from the sky at his brother's feet.

"Lord Ludwig is rattled, but he is trying not to show his fear to his remaining men. He has demanded that every remaining villager attend the funeral to show respect for the fallen men. I believe that he will use the villagers as shields for him and his soldiers."

Lion nodded his head. He knew exactly how the deaths had occurred, and it didn't bother him at all. Hopefully Lord Ludwig had dug that grave large enough for the eleven additional bodies that would be crowding it after this evening.

He clapped Drago on his shoulder in silent approval, before they sat near Mouse to plan the takeover of Droildorf Hall. It was an attractive property, and before Lord Ludwig had gained control of the place, it had been a thriving community. They hoped to repatriate all the refugees that were currently bursting the gates at Tremble Castle.

He learned that Lady Rane was a healer. She had found all of the men, and had tended to all of their wounds, including his own. The idea that a tiny woman had, almost single handedly, saved five huge men was almost laughable. That one woman of any size could save a man of his magnitude was completely unbelievable, until Drago informed him of the Rane's discovery of him in the dungeon, and the subsequent events that she, Lord Nord, and Max had orchestrated.

"She insists that she has no title, such as Lady, but when you meet her you will understand the need to honor her as a Lady. Lady Rane has earned her title, and your brother has developed an affection for her like none before. We all owe the woman a great debt for saving our lives."

As Lion listened to Drago recount the happenings of the last two weeks, his mind kept going back to the statement Drago made about his brother's affection for Lady Rane.

She was a healer. Her heart was fierce. Her bravery unquestionable. Could she be the one they had hoped to find? Would she be the one to complete the prophesy? He could barely wait to meet the woman.

****

Nord guarded his lady from his position perched in a fringed pine. His form of a Great Horned Owl, watched as Rane patched up the blisters on an old man's hands. So far she had tended the hurts of three others.

He tensed when three soldiers came into the village to patrol the area, and watched as they rounded up the villagers for the evening's funerals. When they happened across Rane, they insisted that she come to the hall with the rest of the villagers. She tried to politely refuse with the excuse of tending to the two infirm ladies that had caught a fever last evening, but the soldiers wouldn't take no for an answer. They insisted that she be present to honor those that had fallen defending their village.

****

Rane shrugged, and assisted another woman to her feet. She left the two bedridden women on their pallets, and tried not to scoff at the notion that the men who had died had held any honor. The very idea that those horrid men had died defending anyone, especially anyone not useful to them, was a laugh. However, she knew better than to call the soldiers out on their blatant lie.

She looked up into the trees, and on the ground, but did not see Nord. He had promised her that she could continue to tend to the old people in the village as long as they stayed, or until Lion awakened and had another plan. He was supposed to return before dark to escort her back to the cave.

Hopefully, Lord Nord would not be too upset with her over this. It wasn't as though she had a choice. The soldiers could easily overpower her, plus she couldn't let the older villagers go to this gathering alone. Lord Ludwig would be in an awful temper, and someone needed to protect the innocent and frail.

As they passed the spot where her hovel had stood, she stopped and said a short prayer to the Goddess. She mourned the medicinal supplies, as well as, the little shelter that had been the only home she had ever known. At least she still had her memories of Old Erma.

Simon would likely be at this gathering, and she prayed for strength to fight him off. She hadn't forgotten his threats.

After what Nord had given her last night, there was no way she would allow Simon to touch her in any manner. She would defend herself by any means necessary. They reached the spot where a wide, deep hole had been dug into the ground. The villagers stood in a small semi-circle around the hole, and watched as ten covered bodies were lowered into the hole on top of a thick pile of dry branches.

Ten? Rane only knew of four being killed.

After the bodies were settled into their grave, Lord Ludwig came out of the hall flanked by four of his henchmen. They all looked to the sky nervously, and Rane wondered what they were looking for. When they reached the small gathering of the elderly, and her, they began to grab villagers and place them between each soldier, with Rane and three others surrounding Ludwig.

This did not bode well for the common people. They were being used as shields. Shields from what was the question?

Lord Ludwig began his speech, extolling the virtues of each man as though they were priests, instead of the corrupt, fools that they had actually been. Even as delusional as the lord seemed to be concerning the integrity of the dead, he spoke eloquently.

Rane gasped when he spoke of his love for his brother. She had not known that Simon was one of the shrouded bodies. The lord gave her a sympathetic look as if he thought she actually cared for the evil bastard.

Lord Ludwig tossed the first torch into the pit, then each soldier followed suit. The men gathered around Ludwig as they walked back into the hall, leaving the villagers standing around wondering if they could go back to their homes.

Della came around the building, barely keeping herself upright, carrying a small bundle of cloth. As she drew near, Rane could see that the girl had been badly beaten. Her face was a mess of bruises, and one eye was swollen completely shut.

All watched as Della dropped the bundle of cloth into the pit of fire, before collapsing to the ground dangerously close to the edge of the hole. The girl was only twenty years old, but had been forced to grow up fast once Simon had gotten ahold of her.

Rane knew in her gut that the bundle had been the baby that Della wished to miscarry. The beating must have brought the babe too early and caused its death. Rane went to the girl and pulled her to her feet, wrapping an arm around Della's waist to offer both comfort and support. The entire way back, Rane absorbed the girl's physical pain. Her mental anguish would have to be dealt with on her own, in her own time.

There was a limit to Rane's good temper. She called on the Goddess to avenge the wrongs done to the girl who was little more than a child. Simon was dead, there could be no greater punishment for him, but someone had taken the girl after that and beaten her. That person, or persons, needed to pay for the cruelty.

Rane settled Della in her brother's former hut. Jon had been one of the first to flee with his wife and two children to Tremble Castle. He left his mother and younger sister here, not realizing that Simon would be attracted to Della, or that his mother would be found dead within days of Simon taking Della into the Hall as his mistress.

The place was a mess. Rane shook out the sheet from the bed, finding a thin blanket for Della underneath. She also coaxed a fire from a small pan of coals that she had gotten from the neighboring hut, before taking a dusty bucket, and going to the well to fetch water.

Nord would just have to understand that she could not leave the girl like she was. Until she knew the girl was physically healed, Rane would stay.

The noises coming from the direction of Droildorf Hall woke her from a restless sleep. There were screams and crashes. Rane walked onto the dirt path, seeing the other villagers peeking out of their homes. No one was volunteering to trudge down the path, to the hall, to find out what was happening.

Her mouth dropped open, and she stood stunned, watching Lord Ludwig racing toward her screaming. He was running and crying, as if the demons from Hell were chasing him. It seemed her prayers to the Goddess had brought vengeance more swiftly than she ever expected.

Ludwig stopped when he saw Rane standing in the path. He grabbed her shoulders babbling something about the Gods being after him.

When her hands pushed at him in a panic she felt the pain of the villager's wounds, and the vicious tearing pains that Rane had taken from Della, flow into the man. She didn't try to stop it. His hands loosened as he tried to escape the torture of her touch, but the energy refused to allow him to move away. The high pitched screams coming from his open mouth bore testament to the amount of pain she had absorbed. Now she gave it all back to the architect of the misery and pain.

Rane felt the last surge of negative energy flow through her hands, and her body began to relax. Ludwig, however, was a sniveling mess still standing in front of her, until her hands fell away, then his body collapsed, writhing in the dirt, at her feet.

She looked up to find Lord Nord standing several feet away from them, watching the scene, and she blushed. This was the first time she had ever used her gift to deliberately harm another human being, and she was ashamed. The villagers came from their huts staring at her in awe, but no one approached her.

She turned to leave, but felt a hand on her arm, right before thick, masculine arms spun her around into a strong embrace. No one aside from Old Erma had ever hugged her like they cared for her. She clutched at the shirt he wore, burying her face in the soft material.

He felt so good, and his scent was clean. Something was different about him, but at this moment she didn't care. He seemed larger. Wider maybe. She drew back just a little, looking up and up, until she was staring into velvety, dark brown eyes. The eyes were the same, but the shape of his nose and lips were different. This was not Nord.

Chapter 6

Lady Rane pulled away from Lion, and he allowed her to slip out of his embrace.

When darkness had fallen with no sign of Nord, or the woman that his men called Lady Rane, Lion decided that they would search for them. He could have shifted into one of his many forms, but did not. He needed to conserve what energy he had, but the others did shift, leaving him and Mouse to find their way to Droildorf Hall.

Mouse tried to navigate the rocks, but kept falling. It got to the point that Lion was so frustrated that he sliced into his own wrist, and ordered the smaller man to drink from his vein. The blood would heal almost any injury that Mouse had sustained, and would finish knitting his thighbone within minutes. The loss of blood was minimal, and the results were well worth it.

By the time the two men got to the hall, chaos reigned.

Nord had shifted into his bear form, and was swiping men with his huge paws. The bear's sharp claws sliced deep anytime one of the men got too close.

Fire rained down on another man who had pulled his sword, and was hacking at the air above his head. He was screaming for the Gods to do their worst. He didn't seem to notice when the heavy sword dropped from his burning arm. The arm kept swinging wildly, as the man turned in a circle continuing to scream while he ignored the flame eating his flesh.

The beautiful, grey coated wolf was busy tearing the throat out of his victim, as a handful of soldiers ran for safety.

Lion watched as Mouse transformed into a large, rat like creature, with a knobbed tail and fanged teeth. The creature latched his small forepaws onto one of the fleeing soldiers and climbed on top of the man. When the soldier saw what creature had captured him, he screamed and collapsed dead. His heart had given out, so the rat creature ran in pursuit of another cowardly bastard. It wasn't long before another scream was heard, as Mouse attacked his prey.

Hawk circled a man that no longer had eyes. His deadly talons ripped bloody slices into the soldier every time the bird dropped down. His clothing was in ribbons and, like most the of the others, he begged to be spared. Hawk was relentless, continuing to strike time after time, until he got a shot at the man's neck. When that time finally came, he rose above the man and he left him to pursue another. The soldier staggered for a few steps, and then fell into the burning grave. He never made a sound as his body was swallowed by the flames.

Lion watched as a figure ran around to the back of the hall, away from the one sided battle. He followed the man. When they got to the village, Lion watched as the man grabbed onto a beautiful young woman with long, light brown hair. He felt as if he had been kicked in the gut by Nord. She was the one. There could be no mistake. His heart beat faster at the sight of the little woman. She had to have given him a taste of her essence while she healed him, otherwise, the allure he felt would not be so powerful.

He walked at a faster pace toward her. She was so tiny that the man dwarfed her in size, until she laid her dainty hands on him to push him away from her.

Lion watched, completely transfixed, as the man began to howl and struggle to get away. He was fascinated by the way the tiny woman stood calmly while the man twisted and turned, screaming to be let go. When he collapsed at her feet, Lion wanted to cheer even though the man still lived.

He watched her slowly turn around to look at her audience, to gauge their reactions. When she blushed, and her shoulders sagged in defeat, it made his heart hurt. Was she truly ashamed of defending herself against the hulking bastard that had grabbed her? He couldn't stop himself from going to her, and pulling her into his comforting embrace.

She seemed to welcome his touch, however, he enjoyed the embrace far too much. He might not remember the way she had labored over him while she attempted to heal his wounds, but his body did. His entire body went taut, and his dick hardened immediately, as his blood pumped faster through his veins.

When she gasped and stood back from him, he reluctantly let her go.

Her green eyes widened, and her mouth opened to say something, but Lion had already sensed the coward at his back. He spun in fighting stance, delivering a roundhouse kick to the idiot's arm that had been holding a short sword. The sword fell to the ground, but the man remained standing, despite the new, awkward angle of his arm.

Ludwig stared at the man before him. Lion had known that this was the Lord of Droildorf Hall as soon as he had seen the man's clothing. He could see that the man had resigned himself to his own death. Lord Ludwig obviously wanted to be killed in battle, but he had already deserted his soldiers, leaving them to die, while he ran for cover. This man did not deserve to die such an easy, honorable death. Lion grasped the man around his waist, trapping his arms to his sides, and carried him back to the carnage at the front of Droildorf Hall.

Lion remembered the tales about this man from a few of the refugees that had come to Tremble Castle. How, at one point, he had been so bored, he ordered a man to be roasted over a fire until the flesh melted from his bones. It seemed a fitting end for a petty tyrant. Especially one that intimidated and tortured, instead of cared for and appreciated, the people under his care.

"For the dishonor and harm you have caused the people of Droildorf, you, and all of your men, will die this day. The grave you dug for your fallen will now be your grave as well, and should the demons want your worthless soul they are welcome to it."

Lion picked up the, now screaming, lord over his head, and tossed his body into the middle of the blue flames. He watched the flames burn higher for a moment, before turning away to find his men.

Behind him stood a few elderly people from the village, and Rane. He fought the urge to go to her and spirit her away to his castle. Now was not the right time.

He looked at his men, who were standing in various states of undress. Nord looked intimidating in his loincloth. Hawk and Max wore britches. Mouse had not changed into his human form yet, and now that there were witnesses, he would not change back until he was alone.

Drago walked out of the woods to the small crowd, and stood by Nord. Lion eyed them all, and made a decision.

"I am Lord Tremble, of Tremble Castle By The Sea. These men are my brothers, and their word is my word. I give this hall, its land, and your care to a man I trust implicitly. He will rule this place with a firm hand, yes, but he will rule this place with a fair hand, too.

"It is Spring time. A time for renewal. From this day on, Droildorf Hall will cease to exist, and this territory will now be known as Wolf's Den. My brother, and friend, Lord Max Lupine will be lord of this place. He will build a small fortress to house the people during times of war and strife."

Max came forward with a wide smile upon his face, and accepted his new title and responsibilities with good grace. He promised the small group of people that they would not know worry about their safety while he was in charge, and made it known that their loved ones would be returning soon.

The men and women of the village came forward to great their new Lord, shaking hands, and hugging Max like he was already a friend. Hawk, Drago, Mouse, Nord, and Lion all clapped Max on the shoulder as they filed past him. They left as the morning light began to peek over the treetops.

Rane squeaked as Lion and Nord came up to her, each man taking one of her arms. She looked from one to the other, but they just kept looking straight ahead. She looked over her shoulder, and found Mouse waddling in his animal form, with Hawk and Drago walking behind him.

They walked for hours along a well traveled path. Lion carried Rane until she fell asleep in his arms, then he passed her to Nord. They took turns carrying her until she woke and insisted on walking. When they reached the dusty hovel, they took one look at it and were tempted to keep moving. Unfortunately, it was late, and they all needed food and rest. The shack was barely still standing. With any luck it would protect them from the cool, night winds, but none of them were holding much hope for even that.

Hawk and Max went hunting, bringing back several rabbits, while Nord and Lion found a water source fifty feet from the shelter. The cooking fire was built outside, and several feet away from the hovel, out of fear of burning the dry wood of the shelter if they built the fire inside. Hawk and Nord cleaned and skewered the meat on branches, before leaving it to cook while they went to the stream to wash.

After they ate dinner, Nord and Lion took Rane to the stream, where she made the men turn their backs while she got undressed, and waded into the water. The twin splashes made her gasp, and she placed her hands over her ample breasts before she turned to face them.

She couldn't see anyone on the shore, or under the water, as it only reflected darkness and a few stars. She began to wade back toward the shore, when she felt a hand grab her ankle and tug her down under the water. She only had time for a short squeak before her mouth filled with water and she was left to bob back up to the surface.

Huge hands grasped her breasts from behind, and she could feel a massive erection sliding between the cheeks of her butt, continuing to the small of her back. The hands holding her breasts squeezed the plump flesh, before releasing the pressure. He continued his assault on her breasts, as his pole slid between the globes of her ass.

Another head broke the surface of the water in front of her, and lips kissed her lower belly, as fingers slid up her inner thigh. Fingers strayed into her curly hair, delving into the entrance of her pussy. Two fingers teased her hole rhythmically, with just the tips of those long, thick fingers stretching her entrance, and making her pant. The fingers on the hands holding her breasts began to roll her pink nipples. She whimpered as, lips caressed the tops of her shoulders, back, and the sides of her neck.

A thumb slid through her slit until it found her clit, applying pressure on the little bud. The digit wiggled the underside of her clit and then pushed upward firmly. Her head snapped back and she moaned loudly. The arms around her pulled her bottom half to her knees from the water, easily holding her aloft. Her legs were placed over the man's shoulders, splayed wide while his hands continued to torment her soft, moist center. The man behind her cradled her body in his arms, clasping the cheeks of her ass, bringing her clit up to his brother's mouth.

She missed the fingers tormenting her nipples, but the feeling of that wicked tongue flicking over her clit, and dipping into the entrance of her pussy, pushed every other thought from her mind. When the tightening of her muscles began, she was ready for the freefall of her emotions, and she cried out making her body's demands a growling plea for release.

"Please," she begged. "Please, help me. This feels so wicked, and so wonderful. My body is on fire. I need, I need-" she screamed as she tumbled into her orgasm. A second, softer orgasm surprised her, and she cried out, as her belly convulsed with the intensity of her pleasure.

"Get on your knees," Lion's deep voice commanded her. The men did the same, before he took her hand, wrapping it around the top of his shaft. His cock was so wide; her fingers couldn't touch.

"Place your fingers here, under the helmet of my cock, like this," Lion instructed her, positioning her fingers where he wanted them. "Let your fingers play with the skin there. Now, lick the tip of my cock and take it into your mouth. Yes, just like that love. Oh yes, just like that."

The texture of his cock was so smooth, and so soft, yet it covered a muscle so hard that it amazed her. When she bent to lick the thick tip of his cock, she tasted a salty liquid that was not water from the stream. She licked the small hole, letting the tip of her tongue explore the opening. Then she kissed the entire thick head, before opening her mouth and taking him inside. There was no way for her to close her jaws around the large cylinder, but she found that by sealing her lips around what she could fit in her mouth, she could suck on him, making him moan. She felt another cock nudge her unoccupied hand. She didn't hesitate, before she grabbed it in much the same way she had the first.

The smooth cock in her mouth began to pulse, startling her for a moment. Then she remembered how her own body had felt like it was pulsing before the overwhelming pleasure took her to the stars, so she sucked harder and was rewarded with a gush of liquid squirting into her mouth. She tried to swallow it but there was just too much. She unsealed her lips, and allowed the liquid to trail out of the side of her mouth. It trickled down her chin, dripping onto her breasts.

When the liquid stopped coming from Lion's cock, she ducked her mouth into the water and rinsed the saltiness away. She kept hold of the cock in her hand, and turned to the other one waiting for her attention.

She started as she had with the first cock, exploring the tip and head, but soon the men's moaning gave her the confidence to twirl her tongue around Nord's thickness. She sucked the head of his cock as deep as she could, before pushing it out of her mouth with her tongue. Her fingers on both hands played with the skin just under the thick heads, and the first cock was moved from her fingers after she felt him flinch and shudder.

The heavy flesh in her mouth started the same pulsing as the first, and she held his shaft tight while she sucked strongly until the liquid flooded her mouth and throat. Again, she swallowed as much as she could, but had to spit most of the liquid from her mouth, or drown trying to swallow it all.

She ducked her head and came up spewing water from her mouth, then did it several times to clean the taste from the inside of her cheeks. She began to giggle, holding her arms banded around her waist, before she was hauled up and onto the mossy bank of the stream.

Chapter 7

Rane woke up to a soft kiss on her lips. Opening her eyes, she looked directly into Lion's eyes and felt shy. While he played with the silky strand of her hair that had come loose during the night, he leaned in, kissed her again, and smiled.

"Today we will reach Tremble Castle. Nord has told you that you are now ours to please and take care of as our wife," he takes a deep breath. "Part of taking care of you, includes protecting you," he says, holding up a hand to stave off her indignant, automatic, response. "I know that you can, and have, taken care of yourself, but it won't be enough in some cases. You are a healer. Not a soldier.

"It doesn't matter how brave you are. We need you. We need to know that you are safe," he huffs out an agitated breath, running a hand through his hair. "Hundreds of refugees have flocked to the castle, from four different Halls, and I don't know them well enough to trust them with you. So, when Nord or I can't be with you, you will have guards," he said it as though he expected a fight from her, but she wasn't stupid.

She could understand that things were probably different at Tremble Castle. She might be a warrior at heart, but she wasn't a soldier. She would never be able to protect herself against shifters.

Over a breakfast of leftover rabbit, all of the men sat and talked, feeding her bits of gossip and information. Many of their observations had her laughing until her cheeks hurt. She had never enjoyed the company of men before, and was happy to be included.

It was Lion who told her why they had originally come to Droildorf hall.

"The people are very respectful, but jumpy. If I raise my voice the slightest, I swear I can hear their knees knocking together in fear. We have run out of room, and if people keep flocking to the castle, we will run out of resources to feed and house them all.

"When my men did not return," He motioned to the others, "I set out to find them. Droildorf was the closest. My welcome was not what I had expected. I was attacked before I ever spoke to Lord Ludwig. I took down a few of the soldiers, but one slipped up behind me with something hard and heavy. I woke up in the cave with Drago giving me nourishment.

"We still have three more Halls to investigate before we can relax in the comfort of Tremble again. My plan is to have each of my most trusted men," he points to Mouse, Hawk, and Drago, "take the reins and rule the Halls that we believe are being mismanaged. Each of them has unique gifts and talents, and I trust them with my life."

"Before we leave for the next hall, Nord and I must complete the bonding ceremony with you to keep you safe. I am sorry that you didn't understand the significance of the vows you gave to each of us. Truthfully, you would be ours anyway. It would not matter how we met, or what the circumstances. Our marriage was foretold many years before our time.

"Our country is old, older than any can remember. The sages have always kept a living diary to pass down to the next generation when the time comes. I will have the Holy Man share our history with you sometime soon, so you will understand what we are and what will happen.

"I have found that even the most insignificant words coming from them are worth listening to, and that I had better learn to decipher, and act, on every word from their lips. They warned me of the betrayal at Droildorf. They warned me about the bash in the head with a rock. It was my own arrogance that landed me in the situation that you found me in.

"They did not tell me that we would meet our wife on this journey, but I think of it as an added bonus. Now it is time to make our way home. I want to get there before darkness falls."

****

Mouse came running around the bend in the path, almost slamming into Nord.

"A band of men are ahead, perhaps a half mile from us. I don't think that they are the friendly sort. They look like mercenaries, and they have two captives with them. Both of them appear to be hard used. The leader of the band just gutted one of his own men, and left him to rot."

"This must be the band of miscreants that has been terrorizing the farmers, and villages, around Tremble Castle for the past few months," Lion's grin was so wide it reached his eyes, and he rubbed his hands together as if they itched. "Today is a good day to remove the cutthroat thieves from this world."

Everyone gathered together, and a plan unfolded.

Lion and Nord had told her about the transformation, and what would happen, but Rane still couldn't believe the miracle that she witnessed. Nord was a beautiful, giant sized, white bear. He was even larger now than when he was in his human form. She stroked his soft fur and lay her head over him.

She watched Hawk take wing, and Mouse become the giant rat-like creature. His fur was as soft as a rabbit pelt, and light grey in color. His fangs dripped venom that could incapacitate his victim, paralyzing them for hours.

Drago was a creature usually only found in children's dreams. He had shiny scales and a forked tale. His large brown eyes looked around the small party, giving a slight nod, before he flew off in the direction Mouse had come from.

Lion was the shifter that had her most transfixed. Where the giant man had stood, was now a beautiful, sleek, massive cat, striped orange and black. He lay on his belly for her to pull herself up onto his back, and her legs were splayed as wide as they could go for her to balance on the wide, muscle covered back of the cat. Her hands couldn't stop stroking the luxurious fur of his neck, and she delighted in his low purr. She also appreciated that he had chosen this form for her comfort. His usual shifted form was that of another large cat, but that feline form sported sharp spikes around its neck, and a long, menacing blade over its spine.

They passed the body of the murdered mercenary, leaving it where it lay. By the time they caught up with the band of men it was well past mid-day. Rane was thankful to be refreshed after a short nap on the furry pillow she rode on.

The mercenaries were laughing loudly, making no effort at stealth, since they had never been seen before. They preferred the cover of darkness to steal and terrorize.

Rane watched as the men walked in pairs or threesomes, spread out across the path. One of the oblivious men in the middle of the trail looked behind him to joke with another, but stopped dead in his tracks, his mouth wide open in disbelief.

The man next to him turned to find out what the holdup was, and cried out.

His companions gasped, as they too saw a beautiful woman, riding a huge cat. The fangs hanging from the beast's mouth were longer than the knives the thieves carried. The cat's head was taller than any of the men staring at the animal.

"I am Rane, mistress to the beasts of the Isle of Tremble. You may give up your weapons now, and be taken to Tremble Castle for a fair trial, or you may attempt to fight my beasts. They will give no quarter to you once I give the command, and each and every one of you will die. What is your decision?"

Rane could plainly see that they were planning to fight.

"What makes you believe that we will surrender to you, or your overgrown cat? Do you really believe that you could overpower, or capture, all of us?" The man who appeared to be the leader of this pack of thieves, advanced towards her while the cat watched his every move.

"I will kill the beast and have you under me within a few minutes. I will teach you were a female belongs. Don't worry sweetheart, you'll still get to ride," he sent her a lascivious wink, letting her know exactly what he wanted her to ride. "It just won't be on the back of an overgrown cat, with your skirt above your knees, pretending to be the Mistress of Beasts. The Lord Tremble must be going soft to send a woman to do a man's job. Is that it? He doesn't have the guts for fighting himself, so he sends a woman to fight his battles?"

Rane felt the tension in the muscles beneath her thighs. For the plan to work correctly, she needed to draw as many men as she could, as close to her as possible.

"I advise you to step no closer," she motioned down to Lion. "My friend does not like you, and when he does not like someone he lets them know in a very painful way. Again, I advise you to put down your weapons, and go to Tremble Castle to be tried for your crimes."

The unwashed, over confident, thief came closer, raising his sword.

"No, witch. Why don't you, and your cat, join us," his tone suggested that it wasn't an actual choice. "We meet up with the rest of my men tomorrow, and you can tell us all we need to know about the lord of Tremble. We will swarm the castle, just as we've planned, but with the information we get from his personal witch," he motions to Rane. "There's no way he won't be defeated. Come witch. We must meet with the others at Rock Cross. You can come as my mistress, or my slave. Choose wisely."

The leader, and his men, were finally close enough.

A scream from the back of the small crowd pulled the leader's attention for a second. It was just long enough for thick, white, fur covered paws to pluck her from the back of the cat, and perch her high in a sturdy tree beside the path.

The battle between the shifters and the mercenaries was short and bloody. Two mercenaries were left alive so that they could be interrogated, the leader, and a coward who had rolled himself into a ball.

The two captives were led away from the scene to be tended to by Rane and Mouse. Rane ran her hands over the woman and found her to be pregnant, as well as being, in a great deal of pain from a dislocated shoulder, and multiple rapes. The girl wanted no part of the large rat, and kept whimpering in fear all the while Rane healed the worst of her, physical, injuries. It was times like these that Rane wished that she could heal emotional damage, too.

The man was basically blind due to the severity of the trauma to his eyes. He could not see what was going on, and was obviously, and justifiably, afraid to voice his concerns. Rane could imagine that he did not want to draw attention to himself. She went to him, asking him to sit down so that she could help him. The man resisted, but Mouse placed his front paws on the man's thin shoulders, and pushed him to his knees.

This man was in serious pain. He had been beaten, and raped by the mercenaries. The girl was his wife. The couple had been grabbed as they were making their way to Tremble Castle from Gorgile Hall.

They told the tale of falling asleep by a pond, and awakening to the sight of a horde of men.

When the husband fought to fend off the attackers, they beat him into submission, before they shamed him by making his wife watch as he was used by man after man. When they were done with him, he was left in a heap tethered to a tree while they raped her. He felt so ashamed, and embarrassed, that he hadn't fought the men to his death. His wife was quick to reassure him that he was no less of a man in her eyes, he had fought, and they were safe now. They vowed to never speak of it again.

Rane ran to Lion, requesting a favor in the ear of the large cat. The answer was given with a nod of his shaggy head. The prisoners were brought to where the former captives sat huddled together.

The man's eyes were less swollen after Rane healed him. Now he could see through small slits where the swelling had gone down. He looked from the massive cat, to the small woman with awe, and accepted the short sword that she offered him with dignity.

As he approached the leader of the scum, all he could see was the man's laughing face as he taunted him, ridiculed him, beat him, raped him, raped his wife. He lifted the sword high, before stabbing it down into the evil bastard's chest. He must have stabbed the man fifty times, before his wife came from behind. She put her arms around him, and talked soothingly. She placed her hand over his, relieving him of the short sword, before the two moved away from the assemblage. They took refuge under a tree, holding each other, and crying together.

Chapter 8

Rane walked between Lion and Nord, as they made their way through the town of Tremble. The other men walked fanned out around them, back in their human forms, while their last captive trailed behind them blindfolded, and scared out of his mind.

Servants rushed out of the castle as soon as they realized that the Lord Trembles were home. The evening meal was served quickly, and by the time the six, weary travelers were full, there weren't even scraps left for the dogs.

"Take our wife to my chambers," Lion instructed his housekeeper, Sivdjia. "Also, have a tub of water delivered for her to take a bath. I want a seamstress to meet with her to take measurements for new gowns," he took Rane's hand, and placed a kiss on the back, before looking at Sivdjia again.

"I want you to pass the word along that Rane is ours. Anyone who even thinks of harming her, for any reason, forfeits their life. She should be treated with the same respect that is shown to me, and my brother. Her words are my words. Do not forget."

Lion turned to Rane with a small smile.

"You will go with Sivdjia. Enjoy your hot bath," Lion looked over to Nord. "We have urgent business to take care of. We are going to set guards and patrols to flush out the remaining traitors, and others to meet the rest of the thieves when they meet at Rock Cross," he blows out a breath.

"In two days we leave for Gorgile Hall," Lion laid a kiss on her lips before walking off. Nord was right behind him, but took a moment to blow her a kiss.

Sivdjia led her into a beautiful room. There were two low couches, and several large chairs. A bench sat by itself at the foot of the huge bed. Gorgeous tapestries lined the walls of the room, making Rane want to examine each of them. She could have stood looking at them all day had Sivdjia not ushered her into a small bathing room. The room was situated through a curtained alcove, and had a wooden seated necessary. This was a luxury that most dwellings had only heard of. No braving the cold night air for the occupants of this room.

The housekeeper smiled at Rane, and pulled a flat metal door in the wall opening, revealing a four-inch hole in the wall above the large, deep tub. Sivdjia picked up a trough, from behind the necessary, and placed it under the hole in the wall. She then yelled into the hole, and within seconds steaming water came sluicing down the trough and into the tub, as Rane squealed in delight.

Wasting no time, Rane looked around to make certain she was alone with the housekeeper, before she pulled her thin dress from her body. She stuck her toe into the water that already filled the tub half way. The water was hot, but welcoming to her sore muscles. She thanked Sivdjia for her efforts as the water stopped, and the woman bent to help Rane wash her hair.

The soap smelled heavenly. Not flowery, but more like fresh cut grass and mint. Sivdjia left her to soak after wrapping her freshly washed hair in a length of cloth.

"I will be back shortly, Lady Rane. Mind that you do not fall asleep in the tub. As small as you are, you might drown, and I have no wish to be the one to tell the Lords Tremble that their mated wife has perished in her bath." She flashed a dimpled smile at Rane, and left the room.

Rane felt the day's tension leave her body, as the hot water continued to leach the stress from her muscles. The events of the past two weeks played over, and over, in her mind.

The memories of the way both men had made her body sing, and the way her heart nearly burst at just the sight of them, made her squirm in the water.

She still wondered how either of them would fit his cock inside of her body. She knew that it was going to happen, and that the first time would hurt, but given their size differences, would it always be painful? Would her body learn to adjust?

The water began to cool, so she stood up in the tub, holding onto the side, so she could step out onto the stone floor. She wrapped her body in a clean, soft square of cloth, and walked into the large bedroom.

Rane was surprised to see that Sivdjia was already there with three women. All of the women seemed friendly enough while introductions were made. The seamstress, Olive, asked Rane to stand on the seat of a big wooden chair to get her measurements for new garments.

When she turned at the Olive's request, her ears caught the muttered, "Her ass is wide, and her tits rival the castle milk cows."

She whirled around on the chair in time to see Sivdjia slap the girl into the wall behind her. The girl that was now being yanked to her knees by her hair was very slender, and obviously very young.

Rane wanted to tell the housekeeper to let the insult slide, but the child had to learn manners and respect. She was certain that Lion would not put the girl to death over such a small transgression, but the girl had to learn to hold her tongue.

The seamstress looked frightened, and the other girl never said a word. She just shook her head in disgust, watching Sivdjia hold onto the girl's hair and shake it every time she finished a sentence, as if shaking the girl's head painfully would settle the words into her lazy brain.

"This is the Lady Rane," shake. "She is the mated wife of the Lords Tremble," shake. "I have been instructed that her every request, and word, be taken as if it was their own," shake. "I was also informed that any insult, or injury to her would put the person at death's icy door," shake. "Oriel, you have gone too far this time," shake. "Now, you jealous little bitch, do you still wish to insult Lady Rane? A woman who has done nothing to garner your ire but exist?"

The girl shook her head. Sivdjia pulled her to the chair where Rane remained perched, and yanked the girl's head back to look up at Rane.

It seemed that the girl, Oriel, was not as graceless as she first appeared to be. With tears swimming in her blue eyes, she apologized prettily.

"I am sorry to have made an unfortunate jest concerning your attributes Lady. Please accept my deepest apology."

If Rane had not seen the gleam of rebellion in her eyes, she might have mistaken the apology as being sincere.

"No, Oriel, I will not accept such an apology. It is obvious that you do not mean one word that you have said. Your only regret is that you were caught. I am not so grand a lady that I cannot bear a few insults issued by a child such as yourself, but Sivdjia is correct. You should feel fortunate that the Lords Tremble did not hear your insults. They seem to treasure my wide ass, and milk cow breasts.

"You need to learn manners, and respect for other people. If your mother is here, I will wish to speak to her tomorrow. I do not wish to see you suffer, but you risk your life, and that would be a great loss to those who love you. I would wish for friends in this place rather than enemies."

Rane nodded to Sivdjia, who gave a slight nod of approval.

Olive finished her measurements, and promised to have a dress ready for Rane before morning. She gathered her measuring strings and pins, and left the room.

Oriel, and her sister, Madia, also slipped quietly from the room, leaving Sivdjia with Rane.

"Those two have it in their fool heads that the Lord's will take them as wives. They have tried everything, including a few attempts to seduce Lord Lion and Lord Nord. You will get little help from their mother should she come to see you tomorrow. She is the one that helps them hatch their schemes.

"Everyone here knows the legend. They all know that your mating and marriage to the Lord's is fate," she sighed, and helped Rane down from the chair. "Lord Tremble needs to wed them off to men that will keep them in line, and the further away from each other, and their mother, the better."

When Sivdjia went into the bathing room she took the trough and set it on the side of the necessary and the tub, then began bailing the tub out with a wooden pail into the trough. Rane was still amazed at the ingenuity of it all and told her so.

"Oh yes, this is an invention of Lord Tremble's great uncle, many years ago. The man hated using a necessary that so many others used outside, so he had this one built in the room. We have two more downstairs for the castle folk. He was a bit strange, but his strangeness will keep your delicate rear end warm in the winter months."

Rane was thankful for the informative Sivdjia. The woman was a walking history lesson, and knew everything that went on in the castle. By the time Sivdjia left the rooms, Rane was in bed with her hair brushed out, and sweet scented candles burned near the hearth.

As she lay in the huge bed, Rane wondered what the coming ceremony would entail. She also wondered where this new self-confidence was coming from, and was proud of herself for not breaking down and crying at the insults that the girl so thoughtlessly uttered. There was a time, not so long ago, that she would have been hurt by such words.

She fell asleep thinking of how her life had changed in such a short time.

****

Lion and Nord bathed in the downstairs wash rooms. After securing the castle gates and sending out the best scouts that they had, it was time to embrace the little woman as their own for real.

The elders had told them that she would change in appearance once she consumed a few drops of blood from each of them, before the mating was consummated. During that time her body would adjust for her comfort. What that would entail, they didn't know, but it was time to find out.

****

Rane woke up surrounded by hot, male flesh. Each man had a nipple in his mouth, and a finger sliding into her small pussy. Her knees were bent and splayed wide, as the remaining fingers and thumbs tormented her slit, rear entrance, and clit.

She gasped, feeling the pulling at her tunnel. Those thick fingers were pulling in different directions widening her for their cocks. It felt good, and just a little painful, as the fingers went deeper, keeping the pressure steady. The thumbs on each side of her clit rubbed in unison, the feeling was like no other she had experienced before.

Her strangled scream of pleasure seemed to egg them on in their efforts to bring her to ecstasy.

A finger began to work its way into her tiny rear opening, and she gurgled on a moan, while her body tried to pull away from the slow, stretching burn. When the finger pushed through the ring of muscle, she felt as if she was shattering into pieces of light. The suction increased on her nipples, as she gave herself over to the clenching pleasure. She felt her pussy and butt hole grasping at the thick fingers at the peak of her orgasm, and screamed her pleasure for all to hear.

Lion wanted inside her more than he wanted his next breath, but he had to wait until the blood ritual was finished. He, reluctantly, pulled his mouth from her breast, and looked into her green eyes. He had to smile at the beautiful, dazed look on her face.

Nord was still playing in the creamy entrance of her pussy when Lion bent to kiss her. She bit at his lower lip, and when Nord's thumb mashed her clit, she bit down hard enough to draw blood.

She could taste the odd, metallic flavor on her tongue, as she sucked at the wound she had made. The harder she sucked the more pleasure she felt. He pulled back from her before she was finished, and she whimpered for more as she tried to follow his mouth. His lips was coated with his blood, which he allowed her to lick it off, before he trailed his lips down to her breast. Nord then came up beside her, leaning in for his kiss.

Lion lay between her thighs, pushing two fingers into her tightness. He worked those fingers hard and fast, while she moaned and writhed on the bed.

When Nord quieted her scream with his mouth on hers, she didn't hesitate to bite him in the same fashion as she had Lion. Her teeth ground down on his bottom lip. She loved the taste of him, and the feeling of his body covering her, keeping her flat on the bed, as Lion lapped at her creamy pussy.

She let the lip go to draw air into her lungs, screaming her enjoyment.

Then she began to feel strange. Her entire body felt as if a million fire ants were crawling over her flesh, and her scream was of fright this time. What was happening to her? She felt as if she was stretching.

She began to claw at her skin, before her hands were pulled up and over her head, held in gentle, but firm, grips as she bucked and panted. She locked her jaws, and groaned through her teeth, while her body readjusted itself.

Her body actually rippled, like a rock thrown into water, the ripples spread to her entire body. The feeling that she was being stretched and broken raged through her, and she feared that the pain would never end.

She could not see the glow on her pale skin, or the way her eyes turned to a burning, darker green. Her hair was lighter blonde, and she was, indeed, growing taller.

She couldn't see the beauty glowing from her heart, but the men with her saw it. They saw the future swirling in her eyes, and over her heart. They saw carefree days together, with her at the center of their happiness.

At that moment, all Rane could do was to hang on for the ride that her body was forcing on her. The blood sizzled through her veins, and even her hair felt like it was floating around in the air. There was no place on her body that didn't feel tingly and hot.

Suddenly, the pain and tingles were gone. She could breathe, and move her limbs, without discomfort. Seconds later, another need raged through her. She surprised the men by rolling over on top of Lion, straddling his body. She began to growl and snarl at him, crawling over him, rubbing her body everywhere she could reach.

She looked at Nord, growling at him, and wiggling her ass in the air, as she tossed her hair. He responded by covering her back with his body, and rubbing himself over her, much like she was doing to Lion.

Nord leaned down and bit her ass, then licked the small sting, before traveling down to her soaked slit and licking her cream. He slid his tongue up her slit to her asshole, stabbing at the small, tight hole. His warmth left as he grabbed a small bottle of oil from the table next to the bed.

She felt the trickle of oil being poured on her puckered hole, and shivered in anticipation. Her hands were on Lion's upper arms, holding him down, as she licked and bit at his muscles, purring and rubbing her breasts over his chest. Her lips closed over his shoulder, sucking strongly, as she felt Nord's finger sliding in and out of her smallest opening.

When he added a second finger, she felt the slight burn, and bit down on the flesh in her mouth, making a strangled sound as the fingers went deeper, stretching her wider. Her hips began to move uncontrollably, pushing back on the fingers that were going deeper with each jerk of her hips.

Nord pulled his fingers from her body and shuddered. Knowing that his cock would soon be bathed in the heat of her tiny hole, being squeezed as though it was in a vice, made him hope he would last long enough to feel her pleasure clamping down on him, strangling the juice from his cock. He lifted her legs, spreading them wider, and brought her asshole to the tip of his cock. He positioned her over Lion's thick, straight cock that was, obviously, ready for the warmth of her wet pussy.

He dropped her slowly down onto his brother's cock, feeling her flinch when his own cock nudged at her asshole. The tight ring gradually giving way to the head of his cock.

Her body slowly slid down, until Lion put his hands on her waist, looking into her glowing green eyes, while pushing her hips down onto his cock, breaking through the thin veil of her virginity. When he pushed into her, she screamed, and screamed more, because Nord's cock was buried almost as deeply as his was inside of her body.

Lion pulled his hips down, so she could measure Nord's cock in her ass. His brother was not as long as he was, but he was still large enough to cause pain, or ecstasy, at will. Both of her holes had been virgin, and it gave him a great deal of satisfaction to know that they had been her firsts.

Lion surged inside her tight pussy, as Nord pulled back. He loved the feel of her soft, wet heat surrounding his cock. He grunted as he began to fuck her. When he pulled out Nord pushed in. Rane gasped, and groaned, with each sharp stab of cock.

They could feel the pleasure welling up inside, waiting for the perfect moment to explode into pleasure.

Nord sank his fangs into the side of her neck, as his hips moved faster in counterpoint to Lion's.

Lion came in gushing squirts, as Rane's soft pussy clamped down, and her ass clenched. She screamed through the orgasm, as Lion let his fangs sink into the other side of her neck, his cock erupting. His orgasm triggered a second wave of pleasure deep inside of her, still twitching, tunnel of nerves.

Chapter 9

Rane woke up while it was still dark, her men sprawled out on either side of her. The way her body felt, right now, made her wonder if she would be able to walk again. She crawled over Lion's hips, running her hand fondly over the smooth cheeks of his ass. The gods who had made these men must have been perfectionists.

She had to stand for a few seconds, holding onto the bed post, before she was sure her legs were steady enough to get her to the necessary. Something felt strange, and she was completely graceless, as she tried to walk in a straight line, lurching her way across the room. The feeling was scary. What had caused this disoriented feeling? She wondered if the men felt like she did.

****

Lion watched his mated wife stagger, and stumble, across the floor to come back to bed. She was taller. If he had to estimate, he figured that she had grown four inches. Her voluptuous body was still wide in the hips, with breasts that were more than a handful, for which he was thankful.

She would have to learn to walk again with any assurance. Until that time came he would be happy to carry her anywhere she might want to go.

He was ready to pull off his cover when Nord got out of bed and went to her. He picked her up, sitting with her on the bench at the foot of the bed.

"So many new things for you to accustom yourself to. The mating gave you added height, so that your body could accommodate Lion and I when we make love to our wife. That is just one of the changes that will give you problems at times, until you are used to it. You will also know when we are near, or in need. Just as we will know when you are in need, or near. While I have not heard of it before, you might be lucky enough to change from your human form into one of our animals. But I'm sure it would take more than one blooding for that to happen.

"Lion and I spoke briefly with one of the historians of Tremble Isle last evening. He told us that your body could change again if you carry a large babe, or two. Also, your life span is now as long as ours. So you see, love, we will have many years to love you, and for you to play at bossing us around. However, the next time you allow yourself to be put in danger, as you did back at Droildorf Hall when the soldiers came, I will paddle your sweet little ass, and you will not sit for a week.

"Let me settle you on the bed with Lion. I will fetch some warm water to clean you up and make you more comfortable."

Lion sat up in the bed, pulling her onto his lap, and covering her longer legs. He cuddled her close, thinking she might drift back to sleep, but her questions began immediately.

"How many animals do you have?" She asked, as she stroked her hand over his chest.

"Six. My two battle cats are my favored animals. My bear is not as impressive as Nord's white bear. Don't get me wrong, it's every inch as large as his, but mine is just an ordinary reddish brown color. I have a wolf. He prefers to be alone when he hunts, so I rarely take him out, because we are surrounded by many other wolf shifting people.

"My bird is too large to sit on most branches and stay hidden, but is great for long distance travels. It's unbelievably exciting to feel the wind gliding through my wings, and it's a lot of fun riding the wind currents.

"I have a hooded serpent. I am told the colors are mesmerizing to others. I have used it twice to find an enemy. Each time the serpent has fought to remain in form. It does not like to be let loose, only to be confined again, so I rarely take that form. The last time he was out, after the enemy had been dispatched, the serpent took me into thickly piled rocks, refusing to leave the small space until starvation began to set in. Once we gained sunlight, and space, I put him away."

"Wow. What about the markings on your back?" Rane asks, with awe apparent in her tone.

"The markings on my back began as a burning sensation. Each new mark, means a new animal to call. Then all I have to do is see the picture in my mind, and visualize the animal as best I can. That is how I transform from human man, to four-footed beast."

"And Nord?"

"Nord has his favorite white bear, a white wolf, and his snowy white owl. Oddly enough, all of his animals are white. It seems like every ten years he is gifted with a new animal. Mine came every five years.

"The elders say that it is our ancestry that brings on the beasts to rest within our souls. Much of what we know has been brought down through the generations."

"Is everyone at Tremble a shifter?"

"Many of our soldiers are beast shifters. Most are wolves and birds of prey, like Hawk and Max. They are unique in their beasts due to their size, and ability to reason while in beast form. Drago is truly a fire breathing dragon. He is the only one of his kind that we have found.

"Mouse can take on the size, and demeanor, of a mouse. He prefers to share his time with the rat creature you saw these past few days. As I told you, his fangs carry venom that can paralyze his prey, and he is good at using his abilities to intimidate his opponents. He thinks that the rat is more intimidating than the mouse, and rightly so. Yet, the mouse can go places no one else can. He is an unmatched spy, and we are lucky to have him with us."

****

Nord came through the bedroom door carrying a bucket of steaming water, and took it into the bathing room. He came back to the bed smiling, as he pulled her from Lion's lap.

"Come on, love. Let's get you cleaned up, and back to sleep."

Nord stood her in the big tub, using a soft cloth to wet her body from neck to toes. He lathered his hands with soap, and rubbed his hands over her sensitive skin, before using the cloth to rinse the soapy bubbles away. He turned her around so her back faced him, and had her bend over placing her hands on the edge of the tub with her legs spread wide.

"I love the sight of your beautiful slit," he says, as he reverently runs his fingers over the sensitive flesh. "It is so open and inviting."

He put more soap on his hands, pushing a finger inside of her channel, as another finger soothed her butt hole, by rubbing his slick finger over her tight rear entrance.

Rane whimpered when a stray finger rubbed over her clit. Her entire lower half was sore, yet she felt as if she would die if he didn't let her orgasm, preferably with his large cock buried inside of her.

"Please, I need you so," she begs. "My body needs you to make me feel whole. I am falling apart, help me."

Nord licked his lips as he gazed at her pussy, leaking her excitement down the inside of her thighs. He pulled the cloth from the bucket, and dribbled the cooled, clear water over her ass. His fingers helped distribute the water to rinse the bubbles of soap away from her ass and slit.

Two fingers held her pussy open for the water to trickle in and sooth her delicate tissues. When he moved his fingers to her ass, he tried to ignore the way that rubbery sphincter began to clench on his fingers. As soon as the water sluiced over her clit, her thighs began to tremble even more. He couldn't stop himself from giving into the impulse to lean in and lick her clit and vulva.

She cried out, pushing her backside toward him for more, and shifting her feet to widen her stance.

"I could play with this pretty pussy all night, my love. Your body is so honest with its needs. Tomorrow, Lion and I will take you again, so your body will learn to accept the two of us. Tell me, did you like it when Lion pushed his thick cock inside of this tight spot? Did your pussy tingle and weep, as it's doing for me now? You taste amazing," he groaned against her quivering flesh.

"Your tight asshole nearly strangled my cock when it began to clench while you were in the throes of pleasure. It milked the seed from my cock, and I could not hold back after that."

Nord licked her clit with rapid tongue strokes, and pushed a finger inside her wet depths as she came. He rubbed her satiny, white thighs to sooth, and then used the cool water to freshen her pussy. He picked her up out of the tub and dried her with a square of cloth.

Rane felt the bed on her back as Nord laid her down, before sliding in beside her. She kissed him on the lips, then turned over to use Lion's thickly padded shoulder for her pillow. She felt his kiss on the top of her head and smiled in contentment.

She fell asleep still wondering how she could have been so lucky as to find the two men. Now she was mated and wed to both of them, and she could not wait for the days to come. Two weeks ago she had been just another healer in the village, living in a small hut with her dearest mentor. Now, she was wife to the two most powerful men in the entire country.

When she woke, she was alone in the big bed. The sheet beside her was cool on both sides, so the brothers must have been gone a while. She stretched each limb, and groaned, as she felt the small pop of the elbow in her right arm, and then her hip. What a wonderful way to wake up. It would have been even better if one of her husband's was close by so she could slake this need to have one, or both of them, embedded deeply within her body at all times.

She had to roll over three times to reach the side of the bed and sit upright. As she sat assessing her body, she came to the conclusion that being taller would have to have its advantages. Right now, she could not think of one.

Rane stood up, concentrating on keeping her spine straight, and her legs moving forward. This trip was easier than the first time she had tried to walk. She made it to the bathing room without mishap and congratulated herself. She found a light pink dress on the hook beside the doorway and slipped it over her head.

The material was soft, and felt wonderful against her skin. When she looked down, she began to laugh. The dress was far too short for her to wear in public. The seamstress had measured her yesterday, before the blooding ceremony, and now all of that hard work was for nothing.

Rane practiced walking back and forth in the large room, waiting for someone to come looking for her. She was half way to the bed when Sivdjia walked in the room.

"May I say, you look stunning this morning Lady Rane? I see the ceremony has been completed. We will need Olivia to come back and make some adjustments to your garment. Showing your legs in the bedroom, and showing them downstairs, is not the same thing. Let me send a girl to find her and bring her quickly."

With that said, Sivdjia walked out of the room, leaving a tray that was giving off the heavenly scent of food under the napkin. Graceful walk forgotten, she lurched to the bed, hopped up onto the thick mattress, and began to eat. The food was delicious.

Fluffy eggs on crusty bread, with some kind of thin sliced meat that she did not recognize, filled her belly to its limit. She sipped a mug of chamomile tea after the meal, and relaxed on the big bed. Her mind was on the immediate future.

They would be leaving for Gorgile Hall soon. Tales of the corruption from that place came to mind as she remembered the couple from yesterday. It seemed location did not matter when a man's heart was as black as night to begin with.

Lord Loris, of Gorgile Hall, was a monster. From what the couple had told her, he was much like Lord Ludwig had been. Uncaring for any person but himself, and taking what he wanted without a qualm. He was said to have his dungeons full of people that tried to escape the hall, and the village belonging to it.

Women were stripped naked and whipped until they passed out, while their husbands and children watched, helpless to do anything about the punishment. It was said that young men were placed in stocks and beaten, or worse, for refusing to join the soldiers at night.

Lord Loris was elderly and could barely function now. His head henchman, Comwif, was in charge most of the time. The man was said to have learned his evil work from his master's knee. Comwif was indeed another monster. Both, Lord Loris and Comwif, were said to be shape shifters. This worried Rane.

Where she had the utmost confidence in her men to win the day, and the hall, from the evil ones, at what cost that they succeeded was what worried her. The knowledge that her men had not insisted she stay behind warmed her a bit. She would be valuable in this undertaking if someone was hurt beyond a few cuts and bruises. Knowing that they valued her abilities, set her heart to rest. They had confidence in her, and that gave her such pride inside that she had to smile.

Rane tidied the bed as best she could, given the fact that she had to crawl across it to straighten the blankets. Then she looked around the spacious room for something to occupy her time until the seamstress appeared. She found a hairbrush and used it to smooth the tangles from her long hair. She emptied the bucket of water down the necessary, and picked up the wet cloths, draping them over the tub. She picked up her lord's soiled garments, and placed them on the bench at the foot of the bed, and ran out of things to do.

Chapter 10

It was past the noon hour when Sivdjia came to her explaining that the misses, Oriel and Madia, were keeping Olive too busy to come and assist Lady Rane.

Rane could see that Sivdjia was angry. The young girls and their mother were playing a stupid game and would pay dearly if they continued.

"Take me to them please."

Sivdjia nodded and led her new mistress from the room. Finally, someone would set those three women in their place.

Rane noticed that Sivdjia was walking with a limp, and asked what was wrong. Hearing that the woman suffered back pain at times near her right hip, Rane halted her in the hallway, and laid her hands on the startled woman's pain filled hip and back.

"This is something you will continue to feel as the years go by, Sivdjia. Please come to me, or have me summoned, to assist you when the pain gets this bad. You should not be climbing all these stairs or carrying heavy objects like you do. Don't you have helpers to assist you?"

Sivdjia hung her head, unwilling to admit that Oriel and Madia were supposed to be helping her with day to day chores. Their mother, Lottie, was supposed to be working with the head cook in the kitchens, but the woman often complained of various ailments to avoid work. She preferred to lay about until the work was finished, and then pop in as fresh as a daisy, to accept the praises for other people's hard labors.

The pain in her hip and leg was waning tremendously. Sivdjia stared hard at Rane, and both knew that this was the first time in months that the woman could stand without being overcome with pain. Most days she had to sit down to alleviate the hurt.

The next time Rane mentioned that she would ask the Lord's permission to give Sivdjia women to help her with the chores, Sivdjia told her about the three women.

"They have finer garments than anyone in the castle. Lottie insists that she considers herself the Lady of the castle, and if two more spoiled girls exist in the world as Oriel and Madia, I have not heard or seen them. They came from Hien's Hall with the first wave of refugees.

"The people that came with them will hide from the women, in self defense, when they see them. The trek to Tremble Castle was long, and hard. From what I've been told by their unfortunate travel companions, the women refused to lift a finger to help themselves, or anyone else, during the time.

"Now they are being spiteful to you by keeping poor Olive captive to their whims. They know that you are the mated wife of the Lord's, and will do everything they can to make trouble. Beware, Lady Rane."

Rane heard her words, and took them to heart. Sivdjia was, obviously, feeling better, but the burns on her hands bothered Rane, so she also took the heat and pain from those while the woman stood with her.

When they reached the door of the large room where the three women stayed, Rane leaned over and whispered in Sivdjia's ear a request. The old woman looked puzzled, but went back the way she came to take care of the Rane's wishes.

Rane walked into the room unannounced. The nasty bitches were lounging around the room, while the seamstress was busy with a pile of material.

Her sudden presence startled the women, and they all jumped to their feet. Oriel spoke to her mother.

"This is the whore that graced our Lord's bed last eve, and claims to be the mated wife to both men. Do be careful, Mother, she has the Lords Lion, and Nord, wrapped around her sausage fingers. According to that crone, Sivdjia, there is a death edict over anyone insulting her, or causing her harm.

"Look at her, our Lord's would not pick such a cow to mate with, in truth."

The girl turned her back on Rane, sitting back down in her chair, and ignoring the woman. Anyone in the room could hear the rage in her words, but if they happened to miss her tone, her facial expressions and body language were dead giveaways.

Rane ignored the spiteful brat for the time it took to tell Olive to go to her rooms and lengthen any garments that she might be working on for her.

Olive left the pile of cloth, and raced from the room. She gasped in embarrassment, when she was in such a hurry that she ran into Lord Lion. He nodded at her, and she continued on her way.

Addressing Lottie, Rane began with pleasantries. The woman turned her head, pretending that Rane was not standing in front of her.

"Alright ladies, since you wish to play at being ladies of leisure, then I will suggest to my Lords that you need homes of your own to play in. You madam, have raised children with no respect for anyone, and very little respect for themselves. My understanding is that your Oriel and Madia were given the task of assisting Sivdjia with the housekeeping duties?

"I also understand that none of you have once turned your dainty hands to a task. I have been told that you, Lottie, are supposed to be helping with the cooking for the castle folk, but I find you lounging with your two sluggish children, who feel menial labor is beneath them.

"I see an overwhelming abundance of dresses lying on the floor. I also see a pile of clothing that you have deemed more important for the seamstress to take in hand, than allowing her to assist me in sewing a dress or two to cover my naked frame. A true lady of a castle such as this, would know how to repair small rips and tears in their own garments.

"Your child has insulted me not once, but twice. Yet you sit, with that indulgent smile on your face, and allow her to delude herself into believing her fantasy. I had hoped to reason with you, but now know that my efforts are in vain.

"So, when I see the Lord Lion and Lord Nord, I will request their guidance on how to handle three such disrespectful, and ignorant, women."

Rane turned to leave, feeling disgusted at the waste of her efforts. She hoped Sivdjia had found her lords, and that she could get a garment to cover her legs to make her presentable in the presence of the castle folks.

She felt hands closing on her shoulders, and began to warn the person to back away. The screaming that followed the touch would have warmed her had she known it was Oriel. There was nothing Rane could do to stop the flow of Sivdjia's pain into the hands that touched her. The girl deserved some retribution for her attitude, and this small pain was not much punishment for the brat. Until the pain was released, the flow of

106

energy would continue to be absorbed by her assailant.

Rane looked up and saw Lion standing in the doorway. From the look on his face, she knew that he had heard most of the words spoken in this room, and she was glad that she would not be the one telling tales. By their own words and actions, the women had bought their own punishment. From the look Lion was giving them it might be a harsh one.

The screaming finally stopped, and Rane turned to see Oriel crumpled on the floor continuing to whine. Lottie was standing with her mouth gaped open staring at Lion. Madia stood as far away from them as possible, crying in her hands quietly.

Nothing was heard in the room except the muttering from Oriel, as she threatened Rane with all manner of horrid ends to her existence.

Lottie came closer to Lion with her hands held out in a pleading gesture, which he brushed aside.

He stepped up to Rane, and lifted her chin to look into her eyes. Then, he looked down and his eyes widened at the sight of her legs that were not covered. He grinned and arched his brow, while she stood there blushing under his scrutiny.

He leaned in for a kiss that made all the day's unpleasantness go away for her. The kiss gave her thoughts of last evening, and the early hours of the morning. His arms enfolded her, and she felt treasured by the tenderness he showed her, even in front of the hostile audience. She smiled when he drew back, knowing that he would make everything alright.

Rane stood proudly beside her husband when he turned her towards the three women. She had nothing to be ashamed of, and she had what they most coveted. While she could feel a small amount of pity for the women, she knew that they would happily bury her in a shallow grave, never to be thought of ever again. As long as they resided in the castle, she would need to watch her back for knives.

Madia had not done anything to cause problems as of yet, but what if she were of the same bent as her mother and sister? Could she stay Lion's punishments from the girl with any assurances that she would not turn on her at a later time?

"I have heard your threats and insults to Lady Rane, mated wife to both myself and Lord Nord. By your own words, Sivdjia has told you what my orders were, and still you dare to toss careless words and jealousies her way.

"I have allowed you to play at the roles of ladies hoping that you would grow into marriageable females for some of my guard. I truly considered that you might become friendly with my lady and welcome her. Now I see that allowing you these privileges was a mistake. You, Lottie, have done no service to your children teaching them to pretend airs that do not belong to any of you. I remember when you first came to Tremble Castle. You begged prettily, and bragged of skills to earn your keep that you do not possess.

"I have a ship that is sailing for the new continent in two days. Oriel will be on that ship. While aboard you will scrub the decks, or polish the brass, as any crew member would do. If you work without complaint, or manipulation, you will be given ample means to support yourself until you either, find a husband that will put up with you, or employment in whatever capacity you can find."

The screeching that his pronouncement caused from Lottie and Oriel did not faze him. He waited until they stopped caterwauling before continuing.

"My ship, that trades with the Western Continental Coast is in need of a cook. Lottie, since you claim to have the skill, even if none of us have seen or sampled your talents, you will be on that ship as the cook's assistant. From this day forward you will serve in that capacity. Should that not be to your liking, you may remove yourself from the ship at any port along the coast. If you do not work at the duties assigned, the Captain will have orders to find suitable employment for you until you reach the coast, and then you will be put off the ship to make your own way.

"Madia. You have been silent today. In fact, I do not believe I have ever heard your voice. Can you speak girl?"

She nodded, and spoke in a small voice, "Yes, Lord Lion, I can speak."

"Good, I will have to think of a punishment for you since I have only two ships leaving port within days. I will not force two of you on my captains," He turned back to Lottie and Oriel.

"Once you are gone do not attempt to return to Tremble. If you are found within the boundaries of the country you will be sent into the far jungle, where the beasts live. The only thing staying your banishment to that place is my wife, so remember it well."

Chapter 11

Once they were back in their bedroom, Lion told her how proud he was of her for standing up to the women. His apology for putting her in the situation was very satisfactory, and she still felt the tingles an hour later as she made her way to the main rooms of the castle on his arm.

Nord was standing at the long table with four men. They were drawing on a large parchment. When he saw her, Nord smiled and winked at her before directing his attention back to the man who was speaking.

When they were standing beside Nord, Lion introduced her to the men.

"For those of you that do not know, this our mated wife, Lady Rane. You will extend to her every courtesy due to the lady of our heart. She might well save your life in the future as she saved mine, and the other's that went to Droildorf. Do not underestimate her strength or intelligence."

His words on her behalf warmed Rane deep inside. He had faith in her and her abilities. She stood taller, feeling pride in her husband for acknowledging her talents.

Rane was fascinated by the drawings she saw on the parchment. She had no idea how large the country of Tremble actually was. If this drawing was any indication, the country was huge. The island was divided by lines that had been drawn on the map.

She could not read the letters that spelled out the names of each Hall of Care. Perhaps she could learn to read the letters and numbers that she saw. Then she could understand better, and not have to rely on others to decipher things like this.

It was decided that they would leave after dinner to intercept the two bands of mercenaries that would make their way to the castle before tomorrow evening. The scouts reported that the groups had at least twenty-five men each. Both forces were led by wolf shifters, and since the majority of Tremble Castle soldiers were wolf shifters, it was only fair to allow their own soldiers to join in the upcoming skirmishes.

Dinner became a jovial affair, with Lord and soldier teasing each other into laughter and embarrassment over stories of past battles.

Mouse was lauded as the spy extraordinaire, and then teased unmercifully about his rat form.

"That creature inspires night terrors with his dripping fangs, and tiny front arms," one astute soldier stated. The real shudder that followed his words allowed everyone to know that he actually did think the animal could induce night terrors. Many who heard the words heartily agreed.

Nord held up Rane's hand and kissed her arm nearest his mouth. Then he told the tale of her rescuing all of them, without a hint of embarrassment.

"Imagine our small Lady pulling my hulking ass from a dungeon. Without our Lady Rane, and her quick mind and healing touch, our adventure at the hall would have turned out entirely different." Then he talked of the coming battle.

"When we get close to the rovers, Lady Rane will be stashed high in a tree for safety. You will all protect her with your lives. She is more important than any one of us. She goes with us because of her ability to heal the direst of wounds, and her unique ability to know when an enemy is close. She can detect an enemy from his energy. Unlike our beasts, she does not rely on sight or hearing, so trust her if she urges caution.

"We leave when darkness falls, so be ready."

Nord picked Rane up and started for the stairs. Lion was close behind and grinning at her when she looked over the wide shoulder of her transportation. She smiled back then laid her head on the thick muscle beneath her head. She knew what kind of rest these two men wanted to have. Her body had been humming most of the day with anticipation of being held between her men again.

By the time her feet hit the floor she was pulling her dress over her head and tossing it onto the bench, then she began helping her men get rid of their clothing. Lion was naked first, and she dropped to her knees before him. Her hands stroked his cock from the tip of his thick head, to the silky wrinkled sac holding his stones.

Nord picked her up from the floor and held her until Lion got into the bed. She was placed between Lion's spread thighs, allowing her to continue exploring his man parts. She bent to taste the silky skin, earning a deep moan for her efforts. She licked the sac with short strokes of her tongue, before progressing up the shaft of his cock.

She felt Nord's body make the mattress dip, and cried out when his finger slid down the crack of her ass into the slit of her pussy. She could feel the slick cream trickling from her needy body, and rolled her hips trying to sink his finger deeper inside.

He smacked her ass, "Slow down you greedy puss. I will pleasure you at my own pace. Right now, Lion needs you to work on his cock. You have inspired that look of need on his face. My cock will be buried inside this wet heat and we will all enjoy this time together."

His words helped her focus on the task in her hand.

Nord's finger stretched her tunnel for his cock, making it easier to invade the depths of her body. Then he added a second long, thick finger, and pushed them deep. He twisted his hand and reached around to set his fingers to play with her standing clit. The little muscle poked from its hood as he coaxed it with his fingers, while Rane made gurgling noises around Lion's cock.

She swallowed, trying to keep from gagging on the thick meat pumping in and out of her mouth. Her orgasm was building rapidly, and from the sounds the men were making, she knew they were close too. The slow glide of Nord's cock pushing into her hungry pussy only enhanced the pleasure she felt. His thickness stretched her, and kept running over a certain bundle of nerves deeper inside with every push and pull of his cock.

With Lion running his fingers through her hair, telling her how wonderful she was, and how great she made him feel, and with the taste of him saturating her taste buds with musk and his own unique flavor, it was almost enough to make her pleasure complete.

The exquisite torture of Nord's fingers playing on the cream coated, little bundle of nerves that was her clit, combined with the glide of his thick cock over that special place deep inside, made her increase her efforts to please both men.

She tightened her fist around Lion's shaft, taking him as deep down her throat as she could possibly manage, while shoving back and forth on Nord's cock in an effort to bury him so deeply inside of her that he would be able to somehow feel the same pleasure that she felt.

When Lion's hands grasped her breasts, pinching and twisting her sensitive nipples, she tried to cry out, but only succeeded in allowing his cock to venture deeper into the back of her throat.

Her action triggered the pulsing in his cock on her tongue, telling her that he was getting ready to come with her to that glorious place of bright colors and exploding stars.

It was Nord's words that tipped her into oblivion.

"You are so tight on my cock, I want to stay buried to my balls inside your wet heat forever. God's, the way your pussy gloves my cock is perfect. Watching you suck down Lion's cock so deep makes me remember your sweet lips surrounding my own. I am going to come into you now, love. I am going to come so deeply inside of your delectable body that we will remember this time always."

Nord pushed her thighs together and began pounding her hips with his thighs, sending his cock as deep as possible with each stroke

If not for the suction that she had on Lion's cock in her mouth, she might have been shoved off, but she held on and let her body take control.

The tremors began in her thighs, as she felt that rippling deep inside, knowing that her orgasm was there, ready to take her over and she let it carry her along, no longer waiting for the men to reach their pleasure. This was hers, and she reached out with all of her senses to grab it.

Nord lay over her back and she felt his fangs sink deep into the spot between her shoulder and neck, just as Lion released his seed deep down her throat. Seconds later, Nord's cock pulsed and grew thicker as it began soaking her clenching tunnel with his seed.

Lion pulled her up, wiped his seed from her face, and kissed her. He licked his way down over her jaw, finding the spot that he loved. He began sucking on the skin, before sinking his fangs into her flesh. This little woman had wormed her way into his heart without a thought to self-preservation on his part. He trusted her implicitly, and he acknowledged to himself that his trust was not easily gained. Yet here she was, so deeply entrenched inside of him that life would not be worth living without her.

Each time they came together made him want her more. Just watching her walk, eat, or sleep, made him heat up. The thought of going around with a semi hard cock whenever she was near, stirred the greedy fellow from its nest, causing Lion to groan. They didn't have time for another bout of lovemaking.

"We need to get cleaned up, and be ready to leave shortly. As much as I would rather stay right here and make love to you, we need to move from this bed."

Nord moved away first. The last inches of his, semi rigid, cock fell from Rane's body. He moaned when he saw the liquid soaking her thighs, proof of their mating. Just the sight of her pretty ass still in the air, with her thighs still quivering, made him want to sink into her tiny, puckered opening, to bask in the heat of her body once again. Gathering

117

up every ounce of his self-control, he forced himself to leave the bed before his cock overruled his mind.

Rane laid on the bed boneless, and unable to move for a few minutes while the brothers made their preparations to join in battle.

She eventually got up the strength to crawl to the edge and climbed off of the bed, making her way to the bathing room. She found a bucket of clean water in the tub and made use of it. Then emptied the bucket and went back to the room to fetch her dress.

Her dress was on the bed, but next to it was a small set of manly clothing. There was a pair of pants and a billowy sleeved, pullover shirt with laces to close the gaping front. Next to the clothing was a set of boots, and a pair of thick woolen socks to keep her feet warm. She stared at the garments before turning to the men.

"You are giving me men's clothing to wear?"

At the identical nods of their heads, she broke into a happy smile, running at them and tackling Nord, who happened to be closest to her.

"I have always, always wanted to wear pants like you men are allowed to wear. They seem so freeing and warm." She pulled herself up by grabbing the cloth covering his chest, and tugged him down for her kiss of gratitude at the same time.

Then she turned to Lion. He made it easier for her to give him his kiss by bending down, letting her arms encircle his neck, and then standing up while grasping her around the bottom of her thighs to hold her up while they shared a heated kiss.

His smack on her butt broke into her thoughts of sliding down onto his cock, and bouncing like crazy, until she soared. She drew back and stuck her lower lip out until she saw the small, red line on his neck. When she freed one hand to touch and heal him, Nord captured her hand and held it.

"You will take his blood into your body, and then you will take mine. A few sips will do, but if you feel the need for more, drink deeply. This will strengthen our mating bond, and enhance our awareness of each other. Lion and I need this before you go anywhere outside of the castle. So drink, love. Drink and enjoy, as we enjoyed the taste of you in our bed."

Rane stared at the scratch that was seeping a trail of blood onto his shoulder, before she leaned in to lick the small wound. As she moved up to the slit on his skin, she found the taste of his blood to be heady indeed. There was a slight metallic taste, but the spicy flavor was predominant, and she loved it.

Rane was already breathing heavily when Lion passed her to his brother. Her body was writhing in need as she wrapped her legs around Nord's hips and rubbed her breasts over the rough texture of the vest he wore. The whimpers coming from her throat as she latched onto his neck became moans of satisfaction when Lion slid into her clenching heat from behind.

Just the taste of their blood flowing into her mouth stimulated her body so easily, that she instantly felt a need so desperate, she would do anything to have one of their thick cocks inside of her.

Lion pulled his dripping wet cock from her drenched pussy and Nord replaced it with his, making her groan of disappointment turn to a gurgle of happiness. On Nord's downward stroke, she felt Lion at her asshole and relaxed her tense thighs, allowing his thick cock to enter her heated tunnel. The stretching burn of his cock invading her nerve riddled ass, made her whimper as she sought Nord's cock to fill her needy pussy.

Nord's cock rubbed over her clit until Lion's cock pulled almost completely out, and then slammed to the hilt into her greedy pussy. The men took turns filling her, until the pace she wanted became too frenzied to continue the point, counterpoint rhythm.

Both men slammed as deeply as they could go, while Rane threw her head back and screamed her pleasure. Their voices swiftly joined hers, as both men flooded her clenching holes with their seed.

Still tightly held between the men, she felt their cocks soften and begin to slide from her body. She noticed that her fingers were still clutching her own nipples tightly, so she let them loose. The blood returning to her abused nipples began to send painful stimulation through her body, and straight to her pussy. She began impaling herself onto Nord's softening cock, riding out her sudden need, until she lay against his chest gasping for air, while her body gave up the last twitches of the unexpected orgasm.

Chapter 12

Rane sat in the middle of a tall thickly branched Maple tree. She tried to assure her men that she would be fine on the ground but they would not budge. So here she was, watching the battle unfold a short distance away.

As soon as she was perched high in the tree, Lion transformed into the largest, most fearsome cat that she could imagine. The sharp ridges following his backbone, and the hardened plates of fur covered bone covering his front and rear legs, were strange to see as he moved. They flexed as his muscles did, yet from what she could see below, the plates were harder than any shield made.

The mercenaries had already met, and were heading toward Tremble Castle, before the Lord's Tremble, and their soldiers, came upon them.

From her perch, Rane counted fifty mercenaries on the ground fighting, with more in the air fighting against Tremble hawks.

Tremble's fighters were well organized and fought easily together, but the mercenaries were desperate, they were fighting for their lives.

She watched Mouse as he, seemed to be, gleefully sneaking up behind the non-shifters, picking out one, and surprising the man before he ever had a chance to pull up his sword. His front paws latched onto the terrified enemy's ears, before he gave them a rat's version of the kiss of death by dripping his venom into their gaping mouths.

Hawk was appointed her guardian in the sky. Every time she glanced up his large body was circling overhead. Right now he was engaged in a battle with another hawk. It was a vicious scene, with feathers flying in every direction, and the screams of the birds rising to deafening volumes. Finally, one bird fell from the sky. Its wingtip followed the rapid descent of its body, landing fifty yards from the broken body.

Rane stared at the bird still flying. She was certain it was Hawk when his pattern continued to circle her hiding place.

Nord, in his favorite bear form, was leisurely smacking wolves around as though they were bunnies. Once the enemy was down, no matter what form they were in, they were crushed beneath his heavy paws. He either snapped their necks with his jaws, or when he hit them, his paw broke their necks.

Lion was showing off, or having too much fun, to finish the battle and go home. He played with the men in front of him, just like a cat with a tasty mousy dinner would do. He had three men trapped inside a circle. Each time one would try to make a run for it, he would swipe a clawed paw at them, slicing another cut into their already torn flesh. So far, two were lying in the dirt breathing their last, as another one was still trying to fight his way out of the circle of death that the massive battle cat had him trapped in. The last man standing, raised a long, thin sword, slashing at the big cat. Lion just kept stalking him, until the man tripped on a tree root while walking backward and fell, hitting his head. He did not move from there. The battle cat shook his body, roaring loud enough to pause many of the small skirmishes that were still carrying on.

The humans from Tremble came out of the forest and began to gather any mercenaries that were still breathing. The surviving humans would be given a choice, and while that choice was limited to either deportation as a slave, or death where they stood, the choice would be theirs.

Now that the fighting was over, Rane climbed down from her perch. She would be needed to help the wounded, as soon as she could reach them.

At the bottom of the tree, she stood to orient herself to her surroundings. The perspective from above was almost entirely different from ground level. She started walking toward, where she thought was, the site of the battleground.

A rabbit jumped from the bushes to her right, scaring her until she realized what it was. She told herself to stop being such a ninny and get moving. Surely, there would be men that needed her. She didn't doubt that her men were alright. She had watched them until the last minute before she began her climb down the big tree.

Rane heard someone crashing through the thicket of trees, and smiled thinking it was one of her men coming to retrieve her. Her hasty dissent from the tree would save time, just as she thought. The shiver down her back, telling her that danger approached, came too late. She had not paid attention to her surroundings, her only thoughts had been with Lion and Nord, rather than her own safety.

The man that came from the dense brush was not Lion, or Nord. He was one of the mercenaries. His rough shirt, and all around grizzly appearance, gave away his status. The human soldiers of Tremble would never allow themselves to look like this man. They had more pride in their appearance than this. They also wore thick, dark brown, leather vests, with a wheel of beasts decorating the wide back of the garment.

The man appeared to be as astonished to see her as she was to see him. She saw the change coming over his face and turned to run. She only made it ten steps, before he grabbed the back of her shirt, pulling her to a halt. She struggled with everything she had to get loose from his tight grip, but he was much stronger than her. He had her hands pinned behind her back, tying them together with the length of cord from his greasy, braided hair.

"You must be the animal's whore that Lottie was talking about. Well, I know someone who will pay handsomely for Lord Tremble's toy. More than enough gold for me to leave this cursed isle, and make a new life somewhere else. It won't matter which one of us has you. If they want, you back then they will have to pay the price. They will learn the hard way not to leave what they value unprotected, and alone. You can never trust that someone won't come by, find it, and take it for their own."

He bent at the waist, putting his shoulder under her belly, then standing up with one arm holding her thighs to his chest to keep her balanced on his wide shoulder. His grunt, and the shaking of his arm, told her that he would be traveling slowly with her weight.

She struggled in his hold as much as she could. She hoped to unbalance him, and slow him down as much as possible. She was suddenly grateful that the mating had given her the added height. While his arm held her thighs, she drummed her feet into his belly. The more she wiggled and screamed, the more he stumbled and cursed his way through the dense brush. She kept picturing Lion and Nord in her head, hoping that they had formed the mating bond connection that the men had told her about.

She pulled her torso up, trying to shift her weight onto his neck, while lifting her feet at the same time. Then she rolled, taking him down to

126

the ground with her belly landing on his head. She rolled off of him quickly, then rolled again to get her legs under her, hoping that she could make a run for it before could recover his senses.

By the time she got to her feet, he had gotten to his hands and knees. When he shook his shaggy head and glared at her, she kicked him in the temple as hard as she could with the toe of her boot. His head snapped sideways, but he didn't go down, so she stepped back and kicked him in the throat. She kept kicking him, no longer caring where her blows landed. Her screams of outrage were fueled by the fear that he would get up and try to take her from the men she loved.

Strong arms surrounded her from behind, accompanied by Lion's soothing tone. He released her bound hands, before spinning her around, into a tight hug.

Lion and Nord had not gotten close enough to grab the mercenary before Rane had caused them to topple over. The men had stood back, watching as their little mate took matters into her own hands and began to kick the living shit out of her abductor.

They let her kick the man until it looked like she would fall down, before they moved in to comfort her. Lion spoke to her to get her attention, while Nord waited until she was calmed down, before checking to see if she had killed the oaf on the ground.

Lion held her close, cradling her shaking body against his chest. When her shivers subsided, he covered her lips with his in a scorching hot, desperate kiss. Both were breathing heavily when he pulled away.

He looked down into her bright green, shimmering eyes. Even though there were tears shining in her beautiful eyes, he was relieved to see that they held no remorse or shame for what she had done to fight off her attacker. He set her down, his thumbs wiping away the tracks of tears on her cheeks.

All of the panic and fear that he had felt, when he saw her slung over that asshole's shoulder, would need to be released, but that would have to wait for later. Right now, his mate needed his compassion, not his anger.

He pulled her close to his body and rocked her back and forth crooning words of praise into her ear.

"I swear my heart almost dropped from my chest when we saw you struggling with that man. You did well, and I am proud of you. Nord and I were coming for you when we heard your screams. Later, I will want a full accounting of your reasons for leaving the safety of the tree. But for now, right this moment, all I can think of is how thankful I am that you are alive and in my arms."

He picked her up again, carrying her, with her legs wrapped around his hips, her head on his shoulder, and her arms encircling his neck. His hands held her hips as they made their way back to the main body of Tremble soldiers, leaving Nord to deal with the mercenary. Lion was confident that Nord would make certain that that particular threat to their mate would never have another chance to come near her again.

"I only climbed down when I saw that the fight was over," Rane explained, hugging him tighter. "I got turned around coming down the tree, and then he was just there. He knew enough about me to keep my wrists covered when he grabbed me, Lion. He mentioned that Lottie called me the Tremble brother's whore. He planned to sell me to someone that wanted to use me as leverage against you and Nord."

She snuggled her head closer to his neck. Lion would keep her safe.

"All I could think of was you and Nord. I hoped the bond between us was working, but I was too frightened to concentrate for long. I fought him, but he was determined to get enough gold from selling me so he could leave the island and make a new life elsewhere."

Rane wanted to laugh when she saw Mouse terrorizing the prisoners that had been rounded up, and were tied together in a line. His, bottom heavy, body was standing upright as he walked back and forth in front of the men. She felt a twinge of sympathy for the mercenaries, but not enough to plead for mercy on their behalf.

When she got a good look at the men lined up, she noticed that six of them were in much better health than the remaining four. When she asked Lion about the men, he told her that they were sent by Loris, Lord of Gorgile Hall.

"It is a fact, Lord Loris sent half of these men to aid the mercenary forces. The traitorous prick believes that he will get away with this stupidity. He will pay for this waste of men and resources. We will continue on to Gorgile Hall at first light. He will surrender, or he will die. The Halls of Care were set up for the protection of the people, and to maintain order and discipline.

"They were not intended for ego driven, despots to set themselves up as earthly Gods. The temptation to abuse the privilege, and power, of being the Lord of a Hall of Care has become too great for many of the current Lords. I will dismantle the governing bodies of each of these halls, and replace the current lords with men of my choosing.

"This is a large country, with much to offer, and plenty to go around for all. Droildorf was the first of the halls to be restructured. Gorgile will be the second. Then, we will begin touring every Hall of Care until I am satisfied that we have reinstituted the original plan for each of the halls.

"Now be still while I make arrangements for the prisoners to be sent to the dungeons at Tremble Castle. Stay close by me, but please do not interrupt. You may take exception with something

I say, and you should feel free to voice your concerns, but I expect you to wait until we are alone to give me your conflicting ideas."

Chapter 13

A few of the Tremble soldiers were tasked with taking the prisoners to Tremble Castle, while the remaining contingent continued on to Gorgile Hall.

At sunset, they stopped for the night to rest before the coming confrontation with Lord Loris. The hawks provided small game animals for their dinner, and Rane slept safe and warm between the giant white bear and the beautiful striped cat.

Rane had wanted to sleep in their arms, and asked why they insisted on sleeping in their furry bodies. She was told that they always slept as beasts due to the heightened hearing and senses their animals possessed. She had to agree with the logic, after all, it was not easy to sneak up on a cat. Nord explained that bears had even better senses of smell than a hound dog. The thick fur surrounding her kept the dew from forming over her body, and kept the chilly night air at bay.

The first light of morning came much too early for Rane. She buried her face and hands in the long, shaggy fur keeping her warm. She was so comfortable, and felt so secure, that she never wanted to move. The cat's wet tongue, licking from her neck to her cheek, made her giggle and squeal. She got up when that tongue made a second swipe, bathing her chin, lips, and nose. She sat there laughing, as she wiped the cat's saliva from her face.

When she stood up stretching, the big cat bumped her in the chest with his head, causing her to lose her balance and fall backward onto the huge, white bear that was still lying the ground. The 'oomph' sound that came from her bear made her laugh harder.

The sound of her happy laughter was infectious, causing everyone around them, human or animal, to smile. Even the most sober of the soldiers had to smile at the sound of her genuine happiness. It seemed to set the tone for the morning's trek.

By early afternoon the scouting hawks came back with reports of Loris surrounding Gorgile Hall with soldiers. Villagers were being used as human shields, standing in front of each soldier, as ordered by Lord Loris.

As Hawk reported to Lion and Nord what he had seen, they could see that he was upset.

Finally, Hawk could contain his anger no longer.

"Lord Loris has surrounded himself with four pregnant women. He has stripped the clothing from them, and they are being forced to stand before him with spears resting on their bellies. He plans to shove them on the spears if we come too close to him. One of the women is in the beginning stages of labor. I got the information from one of the Gorgile soldiers that were running through the trees to get away from the hall. He was crying because one of the women is his sister. He could not stand and watch her being murdered, helpless to save her. If he had attempted to save her, his mother and his sister's other children would be put to death. He says that he wants to join up with Tremble's forces.

"He, and ten others, are waiting in the forest. They are willing to swear to our cause. Four are wolf shifters, one is a hawk, and the rest are humans. I believe him. When I changed to human, he could have attacked me at that time, but he never raised a hand or weapon. He was actually thankful that we are already heading toward the hall.

"If the man is dishonest, then he is a very good actor. We must come up with another plan. The man, Loris, has no honor. He has small children bound with ropes around their necks. The man is more animal than anyone here."

Nord clapped Hawk on the shoulder, ordering him to rest for an hour before resuming his duties. Then, he and Lion took Rane aside to the river.

They sat on the rocks near the rushing water, talking about the situation until they came up with a plan, and agreed on the final decision.

"Now, love, we have the problem of what to do with our disobedient mate. Can we trust you to stay where you are put, regardless of what you see or hear, until one of us come for you? Or will we have to tie you high in a tree so you cannot come down and get into trouble this time? Now remember, Nord and I already owe you one spanking for your stunt yesterday. The question is, will we come to get you only to find you gone again?"

Lion trapped her close to his body as he talked, making Rane shiver as she felt his hot breath on her neck. Her concern over the promised spanking left her mind, as she gave into the overwhelming urge to bite the skin on his exposed shoulder. She licked his skin then opened her mouth, surprised to feel two fangs break through the skin between her top canines. They penetrated the skin that she had just licked. Almost immediately, she could feel his blood being pulled into her body. She moaned loudly at the robust flavor, and grabbed his thick arms to stay in place.

She felt a set of fangs sink into the flesh of her exposed shoulder, right before a second set of fangs slid into her opposite shoulder from behind. Exquisite sensations flowed through her body as the power of Lion's blood flooded her system. The pleasure was almost too much to take, as her fangs retracted, and she raised her head in a low scream. She didn't even notice when Lion and Nord's fangs left her skin, due to the immediate and overwhelming orgasm that took over her body. The power of her climax was unbelievable.

She came back to her senses as Nord carried her along the path toward Gorgile Hall. When she insisted on walking, Nord allowed it for a short while.

She wanted to talk about what they had experienced together back at the river's edge. She wanted to ask if the development of fangs in her mouth meant that she would also receive an animal form too. Unfortunately, this was not the time to get into a discussion like that. She knew that Nord's thoughts were on the upcoming battle at Gorgile hall. She promised herself to get the answers that she wanted once they returned to Tremble Castle. For now, she would bide her time and wait.

It wasn't long before she found herself perched in another tall tree. Lion threatened her with, not only, the spanking that she had already earned, but with being left behind at the castle on their next takeover of a Hall of Care.

"I care too much to allow you to endanger yourself. I am asking you to behave, to trust Nord and I to stay safe and carry the day. If we are forced to worry about you while we are fighting, then we may not be using all of the senses that could save us from harm." He kissed her thoroughly and climbed down the tree, after extracting her promise to stay put.

She watched as the men advanced onto the hall, where the sea of villagers stood protecting their soldiers without enthusiasm. Once the common people spied the Tremble contingent, they scattered. A few soldiers held position, but the majority of the men tossed down their weapons and went to their knees.

The few who chose to fight were quickly killed. The others were rounded up fifty paces from the doors of the hall, and sat in the dirt waiting to hear their fate. Five wolves patrolled the perimeter of the group, but no one tried to escape.

When Nord opened the doors of the hall, no one noticed the small rodent that scuttled over the threshold, making its way toward the naked women standing in the middle of the room on a raised platform. Nord could see that one woman's birthing water had broken. The evidence puddled at her feet. More concerning was that were, indeed, sharp spears resting on each woman's belly.

The woman in labor gave a strangled gasp, clutching at the underside of her belly, trying to stop the babe from doubling her over in agony. Lion, Nord, and Hawk stood just inside the doorway. They waited until they heard a shout, followed by a man's scream of pain, before they advanced on the circle of pregnant women, gently removing the resting spears from their bellies. They helped the women down, and sent them to their loved ones.

Standing in the middle of the circle was Lord Loris. He was frozen in place. His facial expression showed the horror that he had felt when he realized that the man-sized rat had bitten him.

When Mouse first slipped between the women, he was hoping that they were more afraid of Lord Loris than they were of a small mouse. He had located his target, and knew he could morph fast, as long as he could get between the women without someone screaming at the sight of a mouse.

Luck was with him. He got to Loris's feet, and morphed into the giant rat. The cowardly fool stood looking eye to eye with the rat's large, red eyes and screamed. The bite on his neck paralyzed Loris. All he could do was scream silently, because no other part of his body would function. The man could barely breathe.

****

This time when Lion and Nord came for her, Rane was sitting on the same branch that they had left her on. Her limbs were stiff from inactivity, but she was unharmed. Lion handed her down to Nord, and he sat her down on a nearby log while both men rubbed her legs and arms to get the circulation flowing through her body again.

Nord told her about the easy take-over of the hall. The baby that had been born, as soon as the mother was allowed to lie down, was a boy.

"Even his soldiers were sickened by his acts of cowardice. Only a handful resisted us, and they have paid dearly for their actions. There are thirty soldiers still at the hall waiting to hear their fate. We are questioning the villagers to find out which soldiers are minions of Loris. Those that are liked, or at least respected, if any, will be spared."

Lion was silent all the way back to the hall. The closer they got to the village the more stoic his expression became. His lack of expression worried Rane. She hurried to catch up with him and tugged at his hand to slow him down. He stopped and looked down at her, swept her into his arms for a soul stealing kiss, then put her on her feet and kept walking.

She dropped back and waited for Nord to walk with her. That kiss told her why Lion had gone quiet. He was about to pass judgement on the prisoners. This was not something that he took lightly. Taking the life from another was never easy. It should never be easy, no matter the circumstance. Those that had been coerced into service, might escape death. Those who had only cowered hoping to save their own asses, would be punished accordingly.

Now Lion had another decision to make. Which of his most loyal men should he choose to become the new Lord of this hall? The decision had to be made immediately. The villagers, and the people from the hall, needed a new normal. A stable new existence, free of tyranny.

He looked around the area for a sign, some form of inspiration. Then he remembered the outrage and fierce emotions, that had radiated from Hawk as he had recounted his findings. He smiled for the first time in hours.

He looked around for Hawk, but his search was interrupted by the sound of birds of prey locked in a vicious battle. The screeching that carried over the breeze was ear piercing to those watching from the ground. Feathers flew each time the huge birds clashed together, tearing at each other's bodies with talons and sharp beaks. The birds seemed to be evenly matched in size and intent. Neither one would give an inch in the battle between the two. One of the birds flew straight up, then came plunging back down so fast that the other bird could not dodge the impact when he was plowed into from above. Both birds hit the ground hard.

Only one of them stood up, shaking his feathers out before launching himself in the air to perch high and preen his ruffled feathers.

Whispered words of surprise, and the name Comwif, floated around through the assemblage. He was almost as evil as Loris had been, and no one was unhappy to see his lifeless eyes staring into the sky. The villagers actually cheered to see the bird lying dead on the ground.

Lion grinned. He knew his decision was the right one. He raised his arm over his head, and let a shrill whistle pierce the air.

The huge bird dove from the spire of the hall to stand next to him. The bird became the man in an effortless shift. Some of the villagers stood open mouthed, staring at the tall, broad shouldered man rising from a crouch at Lion's feet. The fact that he was naked and unflinching, caused many of the shocked people to admire the young man's confidence.

A soldier handed Hawk a tunic and a pair of pants. While another handed over a pair of scuffed boots. When he was clothed, Lion took his hand and raised it into the air with his own.

"The people of Gorgile have been hard used by the man Loris. I give this place a new name, and a new Lord today. From this day forward, this place will no longer bear the name of Gorgile Hall. This place is now the Hall of the Hawk's Nest. This is your new lord, Lord Hawk. He will rule the hall with fairness and honesty. He has my ear, and my confidence. Together you can make Hawk's Nest thrive."

Hawk was staring at Lion in surprise.

"You have earned your reward my friend," Lion told the stunned man. He embraced his trusted friend, and smiled. "Someday you might curse my name for saddling you with this place. For now, bask in your fortune. There is much work to be done to set this place to rights."

Chapter 14

They stayed at the hall for another three days while Rane tended to the soldier's, and villager's, injuries and ailments.

Another of the pregnant women gave birth the night before they left for Tremble, and Rane felt good to be using her talent as a healer again. The babe was a tiny girl, born to its human mother and wolf shifter father. The baby was welcomed by her parents with love and tears, and Rane cried with them. She was exhausted by the time she found her spot between her men each night.

The happy party of conquerors made their way back toward Tremble Castle. Everyone was in a festive mood, and anxious to get back to their loved ones. Rane was, once again, riding on the large cat for most of the journey. Nord remained in his human form, insisting on carrying her whenever she thought Lion might be getting tired.

When she attempted to assert her independence, stating her wish to walk, she was told that her stride slowed them down too much. She gave up asking after they refused her requests multiple times in a row. It was no great hardship to ride upon the soft fur of Lion's beast. Each time she dug her fists into his fur to balance herself, the big cat would purr. When she scratched that spot behind his ears, she felt the vibrations of his purring all through her entire body. He finally stopped and looked back at her, causing her to blush. Even on his feline face, the look just about scorched her in its intensity.

When they came to the river, they decided to camp for the night. While the shifters could have made the journey through the dark with no problem, it would have been difficult for the humans to navigate.

Rather than stop with the rest of the group, Lion continued to the water's edge, following the riverbank down a ways, away from the rest. Rane wondered where they were going, when her mount plunged into the river with no warning. She fell from his back, and came up spitting water, and gasping for breath. She waded to the shore and looked around for Lion.

He rose from the water naked, his muscular frame sluicing water as he stood to his full height. He cocked his finger at her, and Rane pulled her sodden clothing from her body, before jumping back into the river to join him.

The cool water sliding over her heated, naked skin, caused her nipples to harden and stand erect. When she waded to him, his hands cupped her face to hold her for a deep kiss. While his lips seduced her mouth, his hands traveled to the white globes of her breasts. His long fingers manipulated her nipples, pulling and twisting them while she moaned, and leaned into his hands.

Each tug and twist of the delicate flesh made her body hum with need. She could not stop rubbing her crotch over his thick erection. She tried to crawl up his body to impale herself on his hard cock, but he was too tall and slippery.

He pulled his fingers from her breasts and picked her up at the waist, carrying her to the soft mossy edge of the riverbank.

He stood her on her feet, before lying down on the soft, flat bed of moss. His hands were folded under his head. His wide chest looking even wider, his stomach muscles contracting as her cold hands rubbed over the flesh of his body.

"I can't believe that you are mine. No matter how many times I touch you, it always feels like a completely new experience," Rane relished Lion's moan, as she ran her hands over his body. "Your broad shoulders, your hard chest," she bent and kissed each nipple, giving each a little lick, before moving down. "These muscles," she said as she traced along his abdominal muscles, "make me so hot. It feels like I'm burning from the inside out."

Lion's entire body tensed as Rane licked and touched each muscle, getting closer and closer to his cock with each swipe of her tongue, and glide of her palms.

When Rane started stroking the skin at the base of his member, he groaned.

"So smooth. Every inch of your body feels like velvet wrapped steel. Well, almost every part," she smirked as one of her hands palmed his ball sac. "These get hard, but nothing like this," she teased as she used her other hand to give his cock a quick stroke.

Lion growled when she abandoned his most needy area, and continued her torturous exploration of his body. She worked her way down each leg, being careful not to touch his cock or balls when she came back up.

When she finished with his legs, she concentrated her efforts on his hips, and the areas surrounding his proud member. When she was almost to her own breaking point, she gave his sac a thorough bath with her tongue, as her fingers lifted the sac and started exploring underneath. When her fingers pressed into the ridge of flesh halfway between his balls and his back split, Lion's back arched and his groan was inspired her to focus more of her efforts on that area.

While her hand was busy beneath his balls, her eyes considered the length of his dick, that was so aroused, it had fallen against his abs, the weight of his erection too great for the muscle to hold it straight up any longer. She started at the base, licking her way up his shaft, her own sex leaking moisture between her thighs. She was so turned on she could barely concentrate on her task.

When she finally made it to the head of his cock, she used her other hand to stand it up, and began to lap at the pre-cum that was steadily leaking out of his slit. She couldn't help her moan of pleasure at the taste of his essence. She wanted more.

Opening her mouth as wide as she could, she took him deep on her first pass. As she adjusted, his cock slid deeper and deeper down her throat. She was nearly mindless with the need to have him spurt his seed down her throat.

She could feel the cream from her own body soaking her thighs, and when she felt thick fingers entering her tunnel, stretching her wide, she sucked harder on Lion's cock. Her moans were muffled by the thick cock in her mouth. When she felt the fingers leave her body she couldn't help her moan of distress, any more than she could stop her squeal of delight, as a thick cock pushed into her begging pussy from behind. She could not hold her pleasure at bay any longer, and felt her pussy clamp down hard around the large cock stabbing so deep inside of her pussy that she would swear he was inside of her womb.

The cock in her mouth swelled even more as she felt his thighs tighten, and a rush of his seed erupted inside of her mouth. There was too much for her to swallow, so she had to unseal her lips, and pull back a little, to allow the extra liquid an outlet.

As she lay across Lion's stomach, with his softening cock still in her mouth, she felt the pleasure building again.

Nord's large hands held the globes of her ass, while a thumb penetrated her puckered hole. His thick cock dragged across her sensitive flesh faster, as she pushed her ass up to take him as deep as possible. When she felt his cock swell, growing thicker deep inside, her brain exploded into beautiful colors.

Her fingers dug into the sensitive flesh of Lion's belly, but she was completely out of her mind with pleasure, and did not notice his flinch. Her scream could not be mistaken for anything other than a scream of ecstasy.

When her teeth closed over his softened cock, Lion grabbed a breast and squeezed the nipple hard. He was thankful that her mouth opened in another scream long enough for him to remove his cock from the reach of her mouth.

She felt Nord's seed flood her pussy, as he collapsed over her, staying deeply embedded in her, still clenching, tunnel. She was shaking and sobbing before her muscles finally melted, and she passed out on top of Lion.

Nord pulled his softened cock free with a satisfied groan, and a gush of their combined juices. He lifted her body onto his lap, and leaned back against the tree behind him. She had become such an important part of his life that to lose her now would be akin to wrenching the heart from his chest, and the testicles from his manhood. She had already attempted to assert her independence, and he loved that about her. It showed that she was not afraid to stand up to either him or Lion.

The brothers let her sleep for a short while, before they woke her up for a quick, refreshing dip in the river. Since Rane's clothing was soaked, Lion went to the campsite where everyone else was making camp, and confiscated a clean shirt to cover her until her clothing was dry enough to wear.

After dinner was eaten, Rane happily snuggled into the warmth of her men to sleep for the night. How she had received such happiness was by the grace of the Goddess, and she gave thanks to her.

****

Their return to the castle was, again, met with cheers from the people. Several hawks and eagles flew over the turrets, riding the wind currents. The feeling of welcome made Rane cry happy tears. Lion took her into his arms, carrying her through the door and into the dining hall.

Food was laid out on a sideboard for those who needed to break their fast. He sat her in a chair, while he and Nord went to get plates of food for all three of them.

Sivdjia came into the room smiling widely. The smile on her face looked strained. Lion could tell that she had some news that would not be welcome.

"Tell me, Sivdjia, what troubles you so much today? Tell me what I need to know. You have my word that you will be heard fairly."

Sivdjia looked at Rane with a worried expression. Then she looked at Lion.

"Lottie and Oriel are missing. The guard went to their rooms, and came back to tell me that the women were gone. Madia is still in the room that she shared with Oriel, but she refuses to say where her mother and sister are hiding."

Sivdjia wasn't finished with the bad news. News that she did not want to share with the three people seated in front of her.

"Sometime before they left they must have gone into your rooms and… they burned a rag doll with yellow and brown string hair in the middle of the bed. There are black smudges spread over Lady Rane's new dresses, and the carcass of a chicken is in the far corner. That's where it must have dropped after it ran through the room spreading blood over everything from a slit throat." Sivdjia leaned closer to say, "They wrote symbols on the walls of the room. Like witches. I left it as I found it so you could decide what to do when you returned. As soon as you see the mess I will have the room thoroughly cleaned."

Rane could not believe what she heard. The women made a doll in her likeness and burned it? They were that unhinged? She stood and walked to the stairs with Lion and Nord right behind her. She opened their chamber door, and stared at the vandalism. For the first time, maybe ever, she felt pure rage. White hot, burning rage.

Something came over her and she allowed it to take hold. Whispered words filtered through her mind, and she spoke the words aloud as she did what the voice in her head told her to do. This attempt at a curse had been clumsy, and it wasn't completed correctly. Now the women would feel the wrath of their own making. They should have known that a witch leaves a part of herself with an incomplete curse. The two females were as incompetent at witchery, as they had been at assigned chores.

She picked up what was left of the rag doll, then she dipped the round head of the doll into the neck of the chicken, rubbing it hard. There wasn't any blood left in the chicken to stick to the wad of cloth, but bits of flesh and feathers did. She stood and rubbed the doll on the walls, smearing some of the dark black smudging on the material.

The sheet covering the bed was the next ruined item in her sight. She yanked it from the mattress, and then she looked around the room for anything she might have missed.

Those with her, stood back and watched her in action. No one pointed out to her that she was glowing. Her eyes were a vivid, bright green, and her hair floated away from her head. She headed out of the door, and walked swiftly up another set of steps, and then another set. She continued climbing, and glowing, all the way to the top of the turret. A blood red, flag with a circle of thirteen animals fluttered in the brisk breeze.

Rane circled the small space, while the three people that had followed her watched from the stairs. While she walked, her words were not understood by the watchers. She moved faster and faster with each turn in the little rock walled space.

"You, who wish such harm, show yourself. I call on my Goddess to protect me and mine. I claim this place as mine. Show yourself evil ones. I command you to show yourself. I call the Goddess of Truth and Protection, to show me your cowardly path."

Rane held the cloth effigy to the heavens. The cloth in her hand burst into flame, and the ashes scattered in the wind. The sheet became a sail, riding the wind current away from the castle, towards the east. The floating, blackened sheet landed on a cliff edge.

"Show yourselves evil ones. Show your cowardly faces. I challenge you. "

As Rane spoke, two figures walked out of a cave beneath the blackened sheet. They stood on the cliffs edge with the wind buffeting against their clothing. The wind died for a few moments, and then blew in a mighty gust, lifting each woman high into the air.

Those watching the scene would not have believed it, if not for the fact that they were watching when the wind dropped from under the women. Two faint screams could be heard as the women dropped from sight.

Chapter 15

Nord escorted Rane down to the sitting room, while Sivdjia directed the thorough cleaning of the master's rooms, and had the cook prepare dinner for the three exhausted people that refused to rest until the bodies of Lottie and Oriel had been sighted drifting towards the sea, before disappearing under the waves.

Rane's coloring was back to normal. The glow was gone from her skin, and so was the iridescent shine in her eyes. Her Goddess had sent her protection.

Neither man could get the image of the way her hair had stood up, or how her eyes had glowed, eerily sightless, out of their minds. Their mate seemed to have powers that no one knew of until now. Even Rane had not known she possessed such energy and power. Her actions had been instinctive. Her faith in the Goddess unshakeable.

After the bed was repaired, and the last black smudge was washed away, along with the chicken blood, Lion, Rane, and Nord retired for the evening.

Rane soaked in the big tub until she was pruned. When she was done, the men emptied the water, while she brushed the tangles from her hair.

The wind had tangled it into knots, and it took a long time for her to smooth the long, soft strands.

Lion went down to the kitchen, bringing a tray piled high with food, and a jug of wine to wash it down with, back with him. They sat in the middle of the big bed, and talked about everything that had happened in the last week.

Rane admitted that she had no idea of her capabilities using energy.

"I have never felt such rage at another person in my life. I hated Lord Ludwig, and Simon, but that feeling was nothing compared to what I felt when I walked into this room. I felt the hatred and evil left over from the women. They wanted to harm the two of you, as well as me. I will not tolerate someone attempting to harm you."

For that sentiment, she got a hug from Nord, and a laugh from Lion. They could make light of her fierceness, she knew that she would kill to protect her men from harm.

The empty food tray was placed on a low table by the hearth. The wine had been drunk, and the three mates laid together in the huge bed talking and sharing stories, before they drifted off to sleep.

Rane woke in the early hours of the morning, when the sun was just beginning to light up the sky. She left the room quietly, and made her way down to the kitchen where preparations for breakfast were well underway.

She was surprised to see Madia, laughing and chattering, with the kitchen staff as she kneaded a ball of bread dough. Rane continued through the kitchen, and out of the door to the castle's garden.

She looked around, cataloguing every plant that would be useful to her. She was pleased that the garden held many of the herbs that she needed. She made a plan to go into the woods to gather plants that could be transplanted into this beautifully tended garden.

As she walked around, she found a small alter in the corner of the garden. It was tucked behind several tall fruit trees and bushes. Someone had, obviously, been using the alter on a regular basis. Dried flowers and herbs were scattered in a nine pointed star symbol.

Rane was not certain what the meaning of the herbs and star were for. There was nothing dark or evil about the small space, so she left it as she found it. She would ask Sivdjia who the healer in the castle was. Perhaps they could work together when the castle folk needed medical attention.

She made a mental note to remind herself to see the healer before they traveled to Milquest Hall at the end of the week.

Her men found her deadheading a rose bush. She was talking to the plant as if it would speak back to her. She let out a squeak when she felt strong arms closing around her waist. Lion gathered her into the warmth of his embrace, and Nord swooped in for a lingering kiss on her lips.

Her heart felt full. She had been given so much that she was just beginning to accept. She had a real home now. A home where she was not considered odd or untouchable. She had two men who loved her, and who she loved more than she ever thought possible. She had no idea what the future would bring, but she was happy.

Lynn Ray Lewis

I love writing Erotic Fiction.
Give me peace and quiet or a set of
headphones and a good music library and i will
write until my hands hurt. Then I will lay in bed
and think of what my characters will do or say
next.

By Lynn Ray Lewis

Jody's Men
Regina's Men
Mackie's Men
Lucy's Men

A Place For Her (Hade's Temple Book 1)

I Waited For You (Guardians Book 1)

Rane's Giants (Tremble Island Book 1)
Hawk's Nest (Tremble Island Book 2)
Demon's End (Tremble Island Book 3)